All of Me, All of You

VANESSA M. THIBEAULT

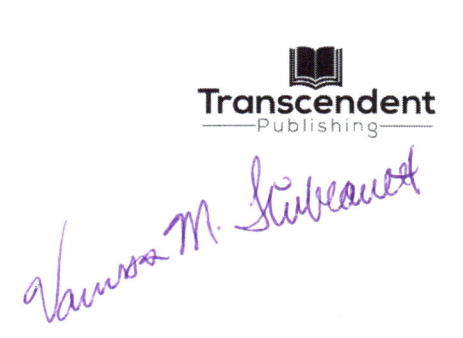

Transcendent Publishing

ALL OF ME, ALL OF YOU

by Vanessa M. Thibeault

Copyright © 2017. Vanessa M. Thibeault. All Rights Reserved. No part of this publication may be reproduced, distributed, or transmitted in any form or by any means, including photocopying, recording, or other electronic or mechanical methods, without the prior written permission of the publisher, except in the case of brief quotations embodied in critical reviews and certain other noncommercial uses permitted by copyright law.

Published by
Transcendent Publishing
P.O. Box 66202
St. Pete Beach, FL 33736
www.transcendentpublishing.com

Transcendent
Publishing

Cover photo and author photo by Jenna Leanne Photography
Edited by Kathleen Marusak

ISBN-10: 0-9987576-1-6
ISBN-13: 978-0-9987576-1-2

This is a work of fiction. Names, characters, businesses, places, events and incidents are either the products of the author's imagination or used in a fictitious manner. Any resemblance to actual persons, living or dead, or actual events is purely coincidental.

Printed in the United States of America.

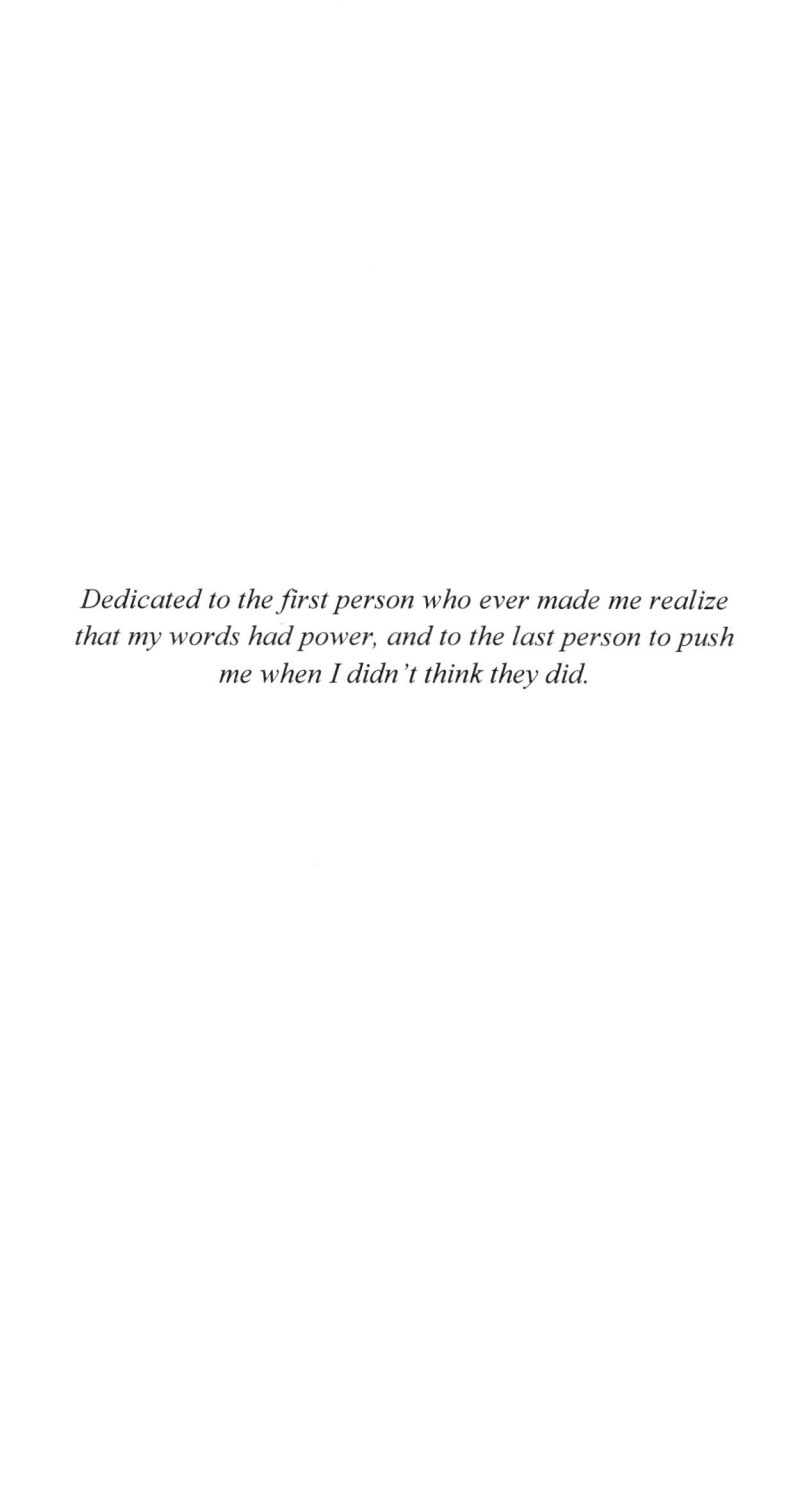

Dedicated to the first person who ever made me realize that my words had power, and to the last person to push me when I didn't think they did.

PROLOGUE

Love. There are times when we just want to grab hold of love and never let go. The love we feel is stronger than anything we have experienced. Our eyes are opened beyond what we feel we can handle. But, sometimes we need to let go of that love. We need to say goodbye and cherish the time we had. Each and every person who comes into our lives teaches us something. Most lessons learned have pain: lessons of love, how to be loved and how to love are the most painful. Keeping an open mind and open heart allows us to let go and to hold on at the same time; an experience so overwhelming it seems our hearts cannot bear up under it, yet, it is necessary. For Emily and Anika, love was both a blessing and a curse. A beautiful mess of two longing souls searching for acceptance and peace in the dark. Although, there is some truth to the adage, "Ignorance is bliss.", when it comes to love, we cannot remain ignorant, and instead must accept our destined path.

VANESSA M. THIBEAULT

CHAPTER 1

"Matisse and I have this game we like to play. We like to people watch. I ask him if he thinks someone is attractive and if he'd sleep with that person, and he asks me the same," Anika said as she brushed her thick red hair from her face and took a long sip of her frosty Corona. A hint of a smile played on her naked lips, humor dancing in her brown eyes as Emily shifted and blushed at thought.

Emily looked down at her hands, condensation and nervous fingers peeling back the label of her nearly empty Corona, just as the weather had peeled the beige paint off the deck under her feet. She was easily embarrassed and like the colour of the bare wood below was visible, so were her feelings transparent.

"Sounds interesting. I guess." Emily cleared her throat and glanced up with bright blue eyes through long blond lashes. She could not help but smile: intrigued, yet, disconcerted. Her face flushed with the lingering thought of the husband and wife, their aroused bodies, Matisse's tongue flicking Anika's nipple while she threw her head back in anticipation of her imminent release. Emily finished the last swallow of her beer. Flustered, she knocked over the pail of water her daughter Julia had left her to guard. Stepping over her clumsy mess, she walked toward the blue recycling bin labeled 'Beer and Wine', willing away the uncomfortable warmth that had spread through her.

"Don't you and Conrad ever discuss who you find attractive?" Anika asked as she took a swig of her beer.

"Not really. No. We don't really talk like that. He isn't interested in talking like that."

"Matisse has joked with me that he'd like to have a threesome with you," Anika stated with a smirk, casually leaning against the railing and looking out into the yard. A slow flush rose up over Emily's neck and face, and she briefly wondered if Anika had initiated this conversation with any of their other friends.

"Ummm..." Emily stuttered and paled. She averted her eyes, looking for a place to concentrate, as flashes of long suppressed desires threatened to make their way to the surface.

"We were just joking, Emily. Relax," Anika reassured still wearing the same smirk. The intensity of Anika's gaze as their eyes met made Emily's face redden again. "Like you've never thought of anyone like that other than your husband?"

"Oh, there's always the short list of celebrities I'd do," Emily laughed awkwardly, a little too high pitched. She winked as she continued, "Like middle-aged Brad Pitt or a young Richard Dean Anderson."

"It's more interesting when you think of average people, though. The ones in your life on a daily basis." Silence filled the next few minutes between the women. The children's chatter reached their ears through the sound of the wind in the crisped leaves of fall.

"Are you okay?" Anika asked.

"Yeah, I'm fine," she managed, struggling to keep her voice even, desire and need threatening to spill out as she tried to hide her true emotions. "You just caught me off guard. I'm going to grab another beer."

"MOMMMMMM!" Children's voices yelled from the other end of the yard. Emily automatically turned in direction of the voices, intending to head down the steps when Anika placed a warm hand on her arm.

"I'll deal with that. Grab one for me too, please."

"Are you sure?" Emily stopped, surprised by the offer of help. Anika nodded, halfway down the stairs, ready to settle whatever disagreement the kids deemed life and death this time. "Thank you," Emily called to Anika's back.

Entering the house, Emily paused with her hand on the fridge door handle. She leaned her head on the cool metal, trying to catch her breath. Biting her lip, Emily sighed, grabbing two beers and closing the fridge a little too hard; a picture of Anika and Matisse dressed up for a work party floated to the tiled floor. Picking it up, her gaze lingered on the seemingly happy couple; Anika's eyes shone and she wore a smile that made her look like she had a secret. Matisse's half smile made him look bored. She returned the photo to its place, securing it with a black and white checkered magnet, and made her way back outside. Anika was just heading up the stairs from breaking up the disagreement between her twin boys about how the swings should be used.

"I'm glad that we were able to get together today. I know we've been meaning to for a while now, but it just didn't work," Anika said, reaching out to take the proffered beer from Emily.

"Me too." Emily swallowed and set her beer on the railing of the beige deck. The women stood in silence, each lost in her own thoughts, until Emily's girls rushing past startled them. While the girls' giggles trailed behind them, their blond hair bobbed down the steps, trying to be the first to the sprinkler, Emily and Anika could not help but let out their own laughter. It was nothing less than chaos when they got together and their five kids played, but both women loved it; it made their houses feel full, complete.

"What are your plans for the weekend?" Anika inquired.

"Not much. Conrad is still gone until Saturday night, so, I'll be trying to get the house in some sort of order. But Sunday we might go to the beach with the kids," Emily replied, as the deep down stirring from before, the warmth which made her so uncomfortable, settled to a dull ache. It would be ignored until Emily could give it her full attention. She wanted to analyze these new feelings. Was it Anika? Was it the thought of the three of them together? Maybe she was just in need of a good old-fashioned fucking. Emily found small talk difficult at the best of times, but at this moment she found it to be a relief. Taking solace in the reprieve her need for answers, Emily continues, "Summer's just about over; we'd like to get a couple more visits in. The girls do love the beach. What about you?"

"We'd like clean up some of the yard and spend some family time together. Do you guys wanna come for dinner Saturday?" Emily watched Anika as she offered the invitation casually, too casually in Emily's opinion given their previous talk of extramarital affairs. Emily once again thought of Anika and Matisse: this time a flash of him fucking her from behind disturbed the innocent conversation of dinner with the two families. Anika peered over at Emily curiously, waiting for a response.

"Umm," Emily stuttered, adjusting the bra strap further up on her shoulder under her shirt, forcing her mind back to the present. "Sounds great. What can we bring?"

"Just yourselves, your kids and your hubby." Anika ran her hands through her thick red hair, raising an eyebrow, a smile playing on her lips. Her plain, yellow gold wedding band caught Emily's eye: functional yet feminine, much like Anika's body. A strand of hair fell from the combed-back mess of Anika's red curls and Emily suppressed the urge to tuck the soft, stray lock behind her friend's ear. Distracting herself, Emily looked out towards the happily screaming children and took a deep breath.

VANESSA M. THIBEAULT

CHAPTER 2

The kitchen was warm as dinner finished up in the oven. The smell of lasagna wafted through the house, making both Emily and her children aware of the hour.

"I'm hungry," Julia proclaimed as she bounced around the kitchen.

"I know, sweetie. We'll give daddy a few more minutes then we'll eat," Emily replied, pushing back the curtains to see if Conrad had pulled into the driveway yet. The space was still empty save for Emily's Subaru. Emily busied herself with the last of the dishes from dinner prep and called Claire to set the table.

"Do I have to?" Claire whined, moping and slouching her way into the kitchen. Complaining, she continued, "I don't want to set the table."

"Yes, you have to," Emily replied. "You live here too. You can help. Make sure to set four places please."

"Fine," was the bored reply that came from her six-year-old.

"Thank you, sweetie." Emily kissed the top of

Claire's head and saw the hint of a smile on her eldest daughter's face. She felt good knowing that the simplest of acts could still make her daughter happy. She turned her attention back to the stove and removed the lasagna from the oven.

6:15. He said he'd be home before six, Emily thought to herself as she looked at the clock again.

"Let's eat girls!" Emily called, placing their plates on the table and piling a good helping of Caesar salad on each plate next to their lasagna. Claire and Julia clambered to the table, excitedly picking up their forks and digging in.

"Thanks for dinner, mommy," Claire exclaimed with a full mouth of salad.

"Thanks, mommy," Julia echoed with an equally full mouth.

"You're welcome, girls, but don't talk with your mouths full," Emily scolded with a smile. The girls chatted about their day: relishing in the facts they learned about the caterpillar's habitat and recounting how the neighbour's dog had not wanted to leave the family of squirrels living in their spruce trees alone today.

"Misty doesn't want to hurt the squirrels, Julia," Emily reassured. "She just wants to play…" Emily's voice trailed off as Conrad came in the door noisily.

"Daddy!" the girls screamed in unison.

"Hi girls!" Conrad exclaimed, sweeping into kiss

them both on top of their heads. "How was your day?"

Emily listened as the girls gave a play by play of the day's events. Conrad half listened, his back to them as he dished up his own dinner.

"Will you read us a story after supper?" Claire asked as Conrad turned around from the stove.

"We'll see," was his short reply as he walked past the table. His excitement for his children having quickly waned. Grabbing his fork and knife, he headed to the living room with his plate.

"What are you doing?" Emily tried to keep her voice even, hoping the annoyance she was feeling was not evident in her tone. No answer came from the living room so she repeated herself louder this time, "What are you doing, Conrad?"

"The game's on," he replied, turning the volume up on the TV. Emily got up from the table and walked to the living room.

"You haven't been home all day and you don't get to see the girls much being away at work. Don't you think you should be eating at the table with us?" Emily allowed the anger and contempt she was feeling to enter her voice.

"You're just about done anyways. They can come watch the game with me when they're done." Conrad's eyes stayed on the TV as he brought a fork full of salad to his mouth and noisily chewed with his mouth opened. Emily stared at Conrad, secretly wishing he would bite his tongue, and walked back to the dining room where the girls were starting to become agitated.

"What's daddy doing?" Julia asked, trying to stand on her chair to see if she could catch a glimpse of her dad.

"Sit down, Julia," Emily curtly instructed Julia. "Daddy wants to eat in the living room."

"We want to eat in the living room too!" Claire cried, jumping down from her chair and scrambling to collect her silverware and plate. Emily reached across the table and pulled her plate from the brink of falling to the floor.

"You need to eat in here with me, Claire. I want to hear more about Misty and the squirrels."

"NO!" Claire stomped her foot and crossed her arms. "I want to eat in the living room with daddy!"

"You need to sit back down at the table and set a good example for your sister. We eat at the table together. And we're not going to argue about it!" Emily struggled to keep from shouting. Her frustration was not with the girls, but with Conrad. She grabbed Julia's cup of milk as she tried to hop down from the table with it, presumably to join her dad in front of the game. "Sit at the table, Julia."

"I want to eat with daddy." She pouted, copying her sister, crossing her arms over her chest, tears welling in her eyes, defiance written all over her face.

"It's not fair if he gets to eat in the living room and we don't," Claire chimed in, still standing beside her chair, moving it back and forth.

"Daddy is an adult and he gets to make his own choices. Just as he has to deal with the consequences of his actions. You are children and you have to listen to me. We're going to eat at the table together," Emily paused, trying to think of a better reason for letting Conrad do what he wanted, but unable to come up with one appropriate for a six- and four-year-old. "Clair, quit playing with your—"

Emily's warning was too late and Claire's glass of milk tumbled to the floor, making a huge mess. Milk splashed all over the floor, up the wall and speckled the legs of the table and chairs. Claire stood with her hands on the chair, looking at Emily, guilty yet defiant.

"Get out!" Emily screamed at her daughter. Frustrated and tired, she pointed angrily toward the stairs. "Now!"

"Fine!" Claire yelled back, stomping off, making her steps heard all the way up the stairs. Emily waited for the inevitable slam of the bedroom door.

"What's going on in here?" Conrad stood in the doorway to the dining room looking in on the mess.

"Nothing," was Emily's curt reply, turning her back to him to retrieve some paper towels and a damp cloth from the kitchen sink. When she returned, Conrad had retreated back to the living room. Julia ate her dinner in silence, watching Emily clean up the milky mess from the floor and surrounding areas.

Going up the stairs to the laundry closet to deposit

the soiled cloths, Emily paused at the door to Claire's room. Taking a deep breath, she entered the room in search of her daughter.

"Claire, I know you didn't spill your milk on purpose, but you have to learn to listen. You can't be bouncing around at the dinner table and not expect something like that to happen," Emily explained, rubbing her daughter's back on top of the covers which were pulled over her head. "I'm sorry I yelled like that. Come eat the rest of your dinner, sweetie."

"No!" she replied from under the covers. Emily sat down beside her and gently pulled back the blankets.

"Finish eating your dinner, sweetie. I put more Caesar salad on your plate." Emily pulled the covers the rest of the way down and reached to pick her up. "I'll carry you down, if you like."

Claire wrapped her little arms around her mom's neck tightly. "Sorry, mommy." Claire's words were muffled against Emily's shoulder.

"It's okay, sweetie. Let's be more careful next time and listen, okay?"

"Okay." Claire's simple response lessened the stress of the situation as they made their way down the stairs. It was difficult to for Emily stay angry with her daughter when she so openly showed her affection.

Emily peered into the living room on her way by to the dining room and noticed Conrad's plate on the table, his half empty beer bottle next to it. Feeling herself start to fume, she distracted herself by kissing Claire's head

ALL OF ME, ALL OF YOU

and gently setting her down on her chair.

"Finish up your dinner and I'll go start you both a bath, okay?" Emily informed the girls, giving them both a smile and taking her unfinished plate off the table. She had lost her appetite. Patting each girl on the head as she walked by, Emily headed toward the stairs, intending to go up and start her daughters a bath. Cocking her head to one side, she could hear water running. "Hmmm," she murmured, sighing and going up the stairs.

The bathroom door was locked, but should could clearly hear the bath water running. "Conrad?" she called.

"Yeah?"

"Are you in the bath?"

"Yep," his reply was short. Above the noise of the running water, he sounded carefree.

"You know the girls have their baths after supper," Emily called to the locked door. There was no response, just the sound of water splashing.

"Fuck you," she muttered under her breath as she went back down the stairs. The girls had finished their suppers and were just taking their dishes off the table. "Daddy's in the bath so I'm going to wash you both up and then we can read stories together."

"Okay, mom," they each replied as Emily washed their faces clean of tomato sauce and Caesar salad dressing. Heading up the stairs, chasing the girls' giggles, Emily stopped as Conrad came out of the

13

bathroom. The girls continued to their room to pick out pajamas and Conrad placed his hand on Emily's hip.

"Want a massage later?" Conrad joked, winking at Emily, still holding onto her hip.

"No! I don't want a massage later!" she replied harshly with finger quotes as she repeats the word massage. "You come home and ignore the kids and I, then monopolize the bathroom when it's their time to have a bath and then you think I want a massage later."

"I'm allowed to relax too, ya know." he replied.

"You could avoid being an asshole when you do it!" Emily spat the words out no sooner than she saw her daughters watching the interaction in the upstairs hallway from their bedroom door. With her arms crossed, she turned to face them, "Girls, go pick out some stories okay? I'll be right in."

"But we want daddy to read to us," Claire stated, still defiant.

"I told you to go pick stories out. I'm not arguing with you. I will be there in a few minutes," Emily curtly told the girls and pointed toward their room.

"Fine." Claire rolled her eyes and stomped away for the second time that evening.

Emily watched the girls turn and go back in their bedroom. Slowly she stepped toward the door and closed it. With her hand on the door handle, she turned back to Conrad. "You need to find a different way to do things. This isn't working for anyone." Her voice was shaking and she had to fight the urge to tell him just to leave. She moved in front of him, challenging his views.

"This isn't something to get upset about," he replied, once again looking bored. He moved to go past Emily and leaned in to give her a kiss as he passed. Her arms were crossed in front of her as she stepped away from Conrad, leaving him leaning down in mid-air. He gave her a curious look, shrugged his shoulders and walked down the stairs

Emily screamed inside her head, screwing up her face in anger and anguish. Composing herself, she let herself into her daughters' bedroom and sat down, bringing both girls on her lap for the stories they had picked out. Emily sighed and allowed herself to be engrossed in the tales that excited her children.

VANESSA M. THIBEAULT

CHAPTER 3

"I can't be with someone who doesn't respect me! I won't raise our children in a relationship where I'm not appreciated or wanted. That's not fair to them and I won't set such a poor example for our children. I won't do it. Something has to change and it has to change soon. I just won't do it any longer." Emily spoke, emotion crowding the words she needed to be heard. Conrad looked up from the TV where he lay on their bed, the sound of sports highlights was barely audible above the sound of the fan in the window. Emily felt herself tense, balling her fists up as the boredom on Conrad's face registered within her mind. Minutes passed before she continued.

"Don't you have anything to say? Do you even care that I'm talking about not raising our children together? Does anything I'm saying make sense to you?" She paused, giving her husband the chance to say something in his own defence, though the chance she is willing him to take is more of a challenge. "I'm tired of doing it all alone and I'm tired of being alone. I work as well and it isn't fair that I work all week and some weekends and I still do everything around here, and with the kids, all by myself. We decided to have these children together and you seem to think you can do whatever you want, whenever you feel like doing it. You only help when it is convenient for you and you never do anything that might screw up what you want to do. You have the nerve to tell me that what I do isn't work and that I should be able to do it all because I'm at home most of the time anyways. I can tell you right now, that 99% of women wouldn't do everything that I do. Nor would they let you get away with the bullshit you pull. Don't you have anything to say?!" she yelled, tiring of talking without being heard.

"Some of what you say makes sense. And I do think you work, but you're home more than me. I'm home ten days a month. What do you expect?" His tone was full of annoyance. His lack of ability to take the conversation seriously evident to Emily by the fact his eyes hardly left the TV to mutter the words to her. "I love you. I love the girls. I don't want to lose you or the kids." Conrad's lanky, dark skinned body was spread out over the bed. His underwear the only cover on his body. It was hot in the bedroom; a September heat wave meant that the prematurely removed air conditioner was missed. The humming fan in the window was making little difference.

"Then why don't you change? Why don't you do something different? I've been talking to you about this for three years and nothing has changed. You keep going about, on your merry way, doing whatever you feel like doing. I want us to get out of debt, but you keep spending like it doesn't fucking matter. I can't be the only one holding this together. You don't want to get life insurance or do a will because you don't like to think about things like that. That isn't being an adult; it's running away from the hard stuff. I shouldn't be the only one to have to deal with what should be OUR responsibilities!" Emily's sweaty palms were the only external indication of the heat in the bedroom, though her reddened face was evidence of the heat of the conversation.

Despite her confident speech, shreds of doubt threatened to creep into her made-up mind. It whispered to her and she faltered in her thinking as the happy sounds of their girls playing waft up from the main floor where they had spread every sticker they owned out on the kitchen floor to find the perfect ones for their art projects. *Am I making the right decision? Fighting this, fighting him?*

She closed her eyes, shaking her head slightly from one side to the other trying to dispel the nagging thoughts that she might be doing this for selfish reasons. The emptiness of the room was loud as the buzzing of the TV righted her thoughts from selfishness back to anger.

"Say something for fuck sakes!" Emily flung her arms up in an act of mock defeat, screwing her face up hoping that it would keep her voice from cracking. So far, she had been able to keep her tears from falling down her hot cheeks. *He'd consider that strength,* she spat in her mind as an acidic thought of her father made her realize just how similar these two men in her life were. She was fighting a similar battle as she had when she was a child, only it was twenty years later and with a different man in a different roll.

If Conrad chose to know anything about her in their ten years of marriage, he should have known what her body language was telling him now. Emily was beyond the point tears. Conrad should have known what it meant for her not to cry. He should have known that she had already made her mind up; already decided what needed to be done and would do anything to see the best possible outcome. When she was able to emotionally detach herself from a situation, she did not need to cry any longer. She simply needed to deal with it as though she was dealing with a problem at work.

Emily wished she was brave enough to just ask for a divorce, but she was terrified of trying to support herself and her children on her own. She was worried about the fighting and arguing with Conrad, which had the potential to become exponentially worse if she refused to cohabitate with him any longer. From Emily's point of view, Conrad had no idea that their marriage was in such turmoil; he had the ability to turn a blind eye very easily, seeing only what he wanted to see. Emily's efforts to do everything possible to save the marriage were going unnoticed, not because she was not trying, but because he did not think there was an issue.

"I dunno what to say. It's hard to say anything when you're standing here telling me I'm such a terrible person. It's hard to hear all the time. Not what I want to come home to. Yelling. Look, I don't want to lose you or the kids. I'll try harder." Emily suppressed the urge to throw the nearest object at Conrad's face. Emily's frustration built as she took in the emotions hinted on his face: indignation for being questioned, boredom, annoyance, but there was something else, too. Maybe it was anxiety, or fear of the thought of losing something he actually cared about.

"Will you this time? Really?" Emily tried to mirror the emotions she saw on Conrad's face, being sarcastic and mocking. Challenging him to attempt the challenge she had set up for him to fail. She had wanted him to change, had begged him to change for too many years. She had allowed herself to believe that at some point things would be different; that she would get better at dealing with the disappointment she felt in the relationship. Emily wished that she had seen his personality earlier; had not tried to escape her past by repeating it, but it felt familiar. She knew how to navigate this kind of dysfunction.

Conrad was engrossed in the TV again. It was hard to tell if the gravity of the conversation had sunk in. If this conversation was anything like previous ones between them, it would never be brought up again. Nothing would change.

"You have to talk to me!" Emily moved, standing in front of the TV, she hoped to garner some sort of reaction from this man. Conrad blankly stared at her, his face showed as little emotion as his words had.

"I don't know what to say. I said I'd do better. I'll do what I can. I can't do anything other than that. I've gotta get some sleep. You know I gotta leave for work in like five hours." The lack of care in Conrad's voice brought tears to her eyes; tears she had been able to keep in check until now.

Relationships aren't about doing what you can when you can; they're about doing what you can when your partner can't. Emily breathed heavily, slowly. Her body wanted to lose control, but she knew she needed to stay calm. Her stomach twisted, she held her fists tight in an effort to keep her voice at a reasonable level. "Do we need to talk more? On a day when you aren't headed back to work in a few hours? Should we try to sit down and make a plan or talk about how we can be better, do better?"

"I don't know what we need to talk about. I think you've said lots. I said I'd do better. Not much else to talk about." Conrad shifted on the bed, pulling the sheet up to cover his body.

I can't do any more, she thought to herself as she willed her tears back. *This was his chance to tell me how much he loved me and wanted me. That he was ready to change. But nothing. Nothing from him.* She sucked in a deep breath. Uncrossing and crossing her arms, she felt defeated. *What choice do I have though? I can't support the girls on my own.*

The muted noise of the TV buzzed in Emily's ears as they stared at each other. Neither one knowing what the other was thinking. Emily had been blunt with Conrad hoping for a better response. His indifference pained her, infuriated her, but did not surprise her in the least; that alone surprised her. It made her question why she was still trying to make this relationship work.

"I need you to change. I need something different." Her blue eyes searched his familar face for any piece of emotion stirring, but once again, found mild annoyance, as he tried to look around her at the TV. "I won't stay. I won't raise them here. I meant it when I said it."

His blank stare finally met her determined one and he rolled over pulling the sheet up around his shoulders. This ended the way all of their discussions ended, with his silence.

"I need to get some sleep," he mumbled from under the covers. "Good night. I love you." His voice was pleasant and childlike as he rustled down further on his pillow getting comfortable.

Emily stood there a moment longer, staring at the blankets moving up and down rhythmically. She shook her head, swallowing hard, the taste of bitterness and abandonment making her scowl as she turned away from the bed and walked out the door. Conrad was already asleep.

VANESSA M. THIBEAULT

CHAPTER 4

Anika walked in with her mess of kids and Emily's house became exponentially louder. Balancing a tray of home-baked goodies, Anika pushed her way through the discarded toys and blankets toward Emily.

"What's in the container?" Emily inquired taking the tray and raising a flirtatious eyebrow. With her now-free hands, Anika ushered the kids through the hallway and out the back door to go play in the beautiful summer-like weather that had continued well into fall. The screen door slammed as the last child ran out, their cries of excitement fading as the wind carried their voices away from the house.

"Mini cheesecakes. Five flavours. Cherry. Apple-ginger. Raspberry. Orange. Caramel. It's a new recipe."

"I LOVE cheesecake. Just pretend you didn't bring any, okay?" Emily winked, pretending to hide the tray in the cupboard. "You didn't have to bring anything, you know. Your company would have been enough."

"I know cheesecake is your favourite," Anika spoke

quietly, smiling, as Emily poured them each a glass of wine. "Thanks for having us over tonight. I really didn't want to stay home."

"Any time! And I mean that! It's great to have the company. The weeks become a little monotonous just the kids and me." Emily held out the glass to Anika. Taking the Gewürztraminer from Emily, she smiled, brushing Emily's hand a second longer than necessary. Emily's heart jumped; she felt herself blush, removing her hand and shaking her head slightly, as if to dispel the unexpected feelings.

Emily had become quite fond of this outspoken woman who had unexpectedly come into her life. Neither woman made friends quickly nor easily. The high standards of conduct they had for themselves were also the standards they preferred in others. Both women had walls around their hearts, but the patience they showed each other allowed them to feel comfortable enough to let their guard down around one another.

Having taken reprieve in the silent house for a few moments, Emily led them outside onto the patio to enjoy the warmth of the extended summer. Emily rearranged the black and white patio set so the two women could sit beside one another. They relaxed in the sun, listening to the sounds around them: the kids playing, vehicles driving by on the highway a few kilometers away, birds chirping their appreciation of the weather. Emily tugged at a stray string on the hem of her capris, her ankle resting on her knee. Holding her ankle with her free hand while her busy hand cradled the wine glass, Emily looked toward the sky and sighed deeply as a robin flew toward the apple tree.

"I'm so frustrated with Conrad," Emily finally said, "It doesn't seem to matter what I say or do, I can't get through to him."

"I'm not sure there's anything you can do to get through to him. He's a narcissist. To him the only thing that matters is what he wants. Everything is always everyone else's fault." Anika adjusted her chair for a better view of the backyard, not looking at Emily as she shared her observations of the relationship.

"I know. I just thought that after all I'd said and done... I just thought that something would change for him." Emily's fingers traced the wrought iron of the railing enclosing the patio. Her eyes followed her hand, as the memory of her fight with Conrad returned. She was oddly aware of how close Anika's feet were to her outstretched ones.

"I understand." Anika reached to give her a hug. Emily drew her hand away from the railing and embraced Anika back with one arm. "If there is anything I can do. If you need a place to stay or a listening ear..."

Emily met Anika's eyes. They were serious but there was something else there too. Emily felt her stomach lurch and her heart flutter. She once again brushed the feelings aside and looked away. Finishing her wine with an unladylike gulp, she reached behind her to set the glass on the table.

"Thank you," she managed to say wringing her

hands in the way she always did.

"What would Conrad have to do to redeem himself? How could he change so you could get on with your marriage? You say you're done, but you have years together. You have your kids. You fell in love with him for a reason; narcissist or not."

"I did fall in love with him. I fell in love with the good parts he still has, but that isn't enough for me anymore. He was and is a hard worker, but beyond that... Everything is about him. And we're probably past that; past him being able to redeem himself. After everything he has done and said, with the way things continue to be even after I said I would leave. To him there isn't an issue; I'm the issue. Does that make sense?" Emily paused, out of breath. She brought both heels up onto the patio chair and hugged her legs. Resting her chin on her knees, she closed her eyes. "Maybe I'm just being a bitch. Maybe I've not given him enough chances. I need to be... I want to be the bigger person. But to what end?"

"I'm sorry, but when the hell is he ever the bigger person? When is he respectful and understanding of your feelings? When has he ever apologized for his behaviour? The definition of insanity is doing the same thing over and over again without a different result. You can't keep trying when he won't." Anika's jaw tightened as she folded and unfolded her arms, finally reaching for her glass of wine.

"In one breath, you're advocating for me to stay and the next, you say I should leave. I don't know which side to take?" Emily teased as she opened her eyes and tried to make light of her situation. "Anyways, I'll quit complaining. You didn't come here to listen to me whine about the choices I've made." Emily placed her feet back on the deck, stretching out her legs. She busied her right hand with the bottom of her pink and blue plaid shirt, open in the front, framing the curves just visible under her tank top.

"It's not you I'm upset with, Emily. He makes me angry. I don't like showing you my anger. He doesn't see what he has right in front of him. It hurts me to see you hurt." Anika leaned closer to Emily, reaching for her fidgeting hands. She squeezed Emily's hand in hers reassuringly, intensity radiating from her now dark brown eyes; eyes that just moments before had been light with happiness, and something else. An emotion that neither women had put words to yet. Emily returned the squeeze and kept hold of Anika's hand.

"You're asking me to remember the years we've had together. You're hoping I can find some common ground and make it work. I don't want to work on it any longer if he doesn't see the value in trying. I know you want me to be happy with him like you're happy with Matisse." Emily put her wine glass up to indicate to Anika to hold her argument, "Yes, you have issues with Matisse and I know it's far from perfect, but the disrespect and lack of effort that Conrad shows me... Matisse would never treat you like that."

Anika nodded, closing her open mouth as she had started to say something. She withdrew her hand from

Emily's to fidget with her wine glass. The women contemplated their conversation in silence. There was a certain disrespect Conrad had for Emily that Matisse would never dream of showing Anika. There were some issues between Matisse and Anika, but nothing they could not resolve.

"I'm sorry," was all that Anika could muster. She looked away, but not before Emily glimpsed the anger on her face.

"Anika..." Emily could see the pain that confiding in her friend was causing.

"I'm sorry, Emily. It makes me angry when I can't do anything to help you. You tell me he ignores you and the girls. That he treats you with indifference and has little regard for your feelings. You don't deserve to be treated like that," Anika spoke in a rush of words. "I find myself having to bite my tongue and not make things worse for you by stepping in where I don't belong."

Emily was taken aback by the sudden honesty from Anika. She had known that the friendship they were building was special, but Anika's feelings for her were stronger than what she had realized. Their concern for one another ran deep. She had not told Anika, but when others had tried to help, telling Conrad to change, it had only furthered his indifference.

"Anika! Don't worry about me, please." Emily was quiet for a moment, reflecting on her affection for her friend. "I fear that I'm not being fair to him. It's not like he's abusive..." Anika gave Emily a harsh, disapproving look. Emily lowered her eyes and stared at the deck. Getting up, she took both wine glasses and headed into the house. Holding the door open for Anika, they made their way past the pictures of Emily's happy family. Emily headed toward the kitchen as Anika detoured to the bathroom.

"He is abusive. Mental and emotional abuse is still abuse," Anika called from down the hall, the click of the bathroom door cutting off her voice.

"I know. I know, "Emily muttered to herself, setting the glasses down on the counter. She paused, hunched over, placing her other hand on the wine bottle. She breathed noisily in and out her nose, gritting her teeth, thinking about how she had defined Conrad's behaviour as non-abusive. Letting go of the glasses and uncorking the bottle, Emily poured the remainder of the wine. Having filled both her glass and Anika's, Emily placed the empty bottle next to the sink. Turning, she opened the fridge taking out peppers, onions, garlic and the defrosted chicken in preparation for dinner.

Emily was silent, lost in thought. She chopped the vegetables and bit her lip unconsciously as Anika entered the kitchen and the background noises of the day continued. Waving the knife she was using to cut up the vegetables for dinner, as if to dispel the notion of abuse, Emily broke the silence.

"It's always something with Conrad. Like the issues with his parents. I don't think it is fair for Conrad ignore the way his parents are with the girls. You expect grandparents to want relationship with their only grandchildren. It isn't fair to the girls, and it isn't fair to us to have to make up excuses why they won't spend time with them. I can't tell a four- and six-year-old that their grandparents don't care enough to call or see them. How do you explain that?" Emily popped a piece of pepper she had been chopping into her mouth.

"That's exactly why I don't have expectations of anyone. If I just do it myself, I won't be disappointed. I've no one to blame but myself when things go wrong." Anika stretched her legs out on the empty chair in front of her. "But what would you suggest Conrad do about his parents?"

"Talk to them. Explain how important this relationship is to the girls. I've asked Conrad to say something and he just tells me he can't make them do anything. He completely believes that it doesn't matter what anyone else does. It should have no impact on anyone else because we just shouldn't care."

"Seems about Conrad's speed," Anika muttered with disgust, then added. "Do you need help with anything?"

"No, I'm good for now. You're on dish duty later." Emily winked at Anika and gave her a teasing smile. "It makes sense, I guess. At least it explains the way he is with the me and girls. He thinks he should be able to do whatever he wants when he wants."

"He doesn't just think it, honey, he does it."

"I know. I know! It is so frustrating, infuriating. I feel like I'm constantly fighting an uphill battle." Emily's tanned face reddened with emotion as she turned to stir the fajita filling that was on the stove. Sighing, she spoke again, looking up at the ceiling, "Speaking of uphill battles, the school finally returned my call about my complaint."

"Oh?" Anika raised an eyebrow. "About the swear words you found written in the grade one books they sent home, right?"

"Yeah. Well, they didn't think it was a big deal. They said they will screen the books better but that they can't guarantee it won't happen again."

"That's ludicrous! You would think they would take more responsibility for what was going on in their school."

"I completely agree! I had an issue with Claire's teacher as well. She was letting the kids watch a movie every week on Friday. They're in grade one and there are a million other things for them to be doing other than watching TV."

"I had the same issue with that teacher last year," Anika replied. "She told me it was a reward for good behaviour."

"More like a break for her at the end of a long week." Emily sighed, frustrated and annoyed by the school's response.

* * * *

The kids were particularly rambunctious at dinner and both Emily and Anika were starting to lose their patience with the constant goofing and very little eating.

Emily was feeling a bit down, still thinking about their earlier conversation regarding Conrad and the direction their marriage was taking.

"Enough yelling, talking and goofing at the table, Claire! It is time to eat, not play around," Emily scolded her oldest daughter harshly. At six years old she knew better than to be yelling across the table.

"Daddy yells at you when you cry," Claire disrespectfully responded to Emily's reminder to behave at the table.

"Pardon me?" Emily asked, her mouth full, forgetting her own manners in the shock of what Claire had just said. Fork in hand, mid bite, she swallowed hard.

"Daddy yells at you when you cry."

"That's enough."

"But he..."

"Enough!" Anika interrupted.

Emily's heart felt heavy. She looked down at her plate and pushed her food around with her fork, no longer hungry. Anika reached for Emily and squeezed her forearm. Emily looked up, meeting Anika's eyes. Emily's eyes were dark, seething with resentment, anger and guilt. She felt irresponsible for allowing her children to remain in a home where their father did not respect their mother. How had she let this happen? She swore she would never let anyone treat her like that, would never raise her kids in such an environment. She had been determined to give them a better example than what she had growing up. She was not going to be a doormat who stayed because she had no other options. She was going to be confident and independent; be a role model for her children.

This will make me stronger, she thought to herself remembering a quote from Mother Teresa: *'I know God won't give me anything I can't handle. I just wish that He didn't trust me so much.'*

Raising her girls was the most important thing to Emily, and the only thing keeping her where she was. She knew Conrad well enough to know that if she started the divorce process, she had better be able to support those girls on her own. He was not going to be kind about the process and he most certainly was not going to make her life easy. They were living together, raising a family and running a household, and he already deliberately made her life difficult. He would make her life impossible, if she did anything to upset the careful balance.

"It isn't any of your business and we're adults. We have to deal with the consequences of our behaviour and you are a child. You need to listen to me when I ask you to do something. That doesn't mean you are to give constant commentary or defend your actions based on what an adult does," Emily spoke to Claire in an even, firm voice, trying to make eye contact with her, but finding it difficult. Anika placed a hand on Emily's arm with concern in her eyes. Giving Anika an apologetic look, Emily continued speaking to Claire. "Do you understand?"

"Yes, mommy," Claire replied sheepishly. "Sorry, mommy."

"Thank you, sweetie. Now eat up."

"Are you okay?" Anika asked, her hand still on Emily's arm.

"I'm okay."

"Are you okay with how I spoke to Claire?"

"Yes, thank you. I wasn't sure what to say. All is good." Emily gave a small reassuring smile, but it did not reach her eyes. It troubled Emily that her six-year-old could be so intuitive when it came to adult issues, but it also made her doubt just how well she was hiding the realities of her relationship, or her unhappiness.

CHAPTER 5

I wonder if that was an accident or done on purpose? Emily thought to herself as Anika's foot pressed against her leg. Sitting at opposite ends of Anika's grey leather couch, the women stretched their legs out under the blanket they were sharing.

Glasses of wine in hand, they were discussing the mini-series, Pillars of the Earth, they had just finished watching together. Three empty bottles of Anika's favourite wine, Mascato, sat on the table in front of them; both women were feeling the effects of their indulgence.

Emily moved her leg to return the gesture. Through long blond lashes, she caught Anika's eye, trying to gauge her response. Anika was hard to read, but the desire in her eyes was impossible to miss; it was present in Emily, too. Anika pressed her leg into Emily's and she felt a flush of arousal and emotion spread through her body. Looking away, they sipped the last of the wine in silence, taking in the presence of each other's bodies so close for the first time.

Visible from where they sat on the couch, the moon

shone through the closed sheers behind them. It was a clear, mostly calm night. The gentle breeze blew through the open window moving the red curtains and giving the women goosebumps. The smell of cool grass wafted in, overwhelming their already heightened senses.

Conversation between the women faded, leaving the room in a silence filled with expectation, desire and the faint sounds of the night. Emily glanced up from her wine to see Anika staring at her with an intensity that made her blush. Anika took another sip of her wine and placed it on the stone and wood coffee table beside her; doing so shifted her body closer to Emily's.

Emily emptied her wine and placed her glass on the table next to Anika's. She pulled the blanket up, though at that moment she was anything but cold, and leaned closer to Anika. Anika's hands were already under the blanket, having found Emily's leg. Emily felt a strong, slow ache rise in her as Anika gently stroked up and down Emily's toned calf. She reached under the blanket to find Anika's leg to return the gesture. Slowly their fingers met, lacing together.

Moving together they wrapped their legs around each other. Their fingertips sent shivers through their bodies as they mimicked the other's movements: a slow trail up their arms and over their shoulders, pausing only to explore the gentle rise of each other's collar bones. Eyes closed, both women touched and caressed the other. Emily had not felt this alive, this aroused in a very long time.

Emily opened her usually light blue eyes which

have darkened considerably and met Anika's brown ones which, consequently, had lightened. Both women wore expectant and needy, yet hesitant gazes. They leaned in allowing their foreheads to rest together, arms around each other. Their knees were pulled up to their chests while their legs wrap around their torsos.

Emily breathed in deeply, attempting to calm her nerves. Pressing her cheek to Anika's, feeling it warm on hers, she realized Anika was just as on fire as she was. Their breathing now laboured, Emily slowly pulled away to allow their lips to come together at last. Both women gasped, their breath stolen from the electricity exchanged between them.

Emily felt tears come to her eyes in a sudden release of emotion. She placed her right hand on Anika's neck, her other still on Anika's back, deepening the kiss. Anika held tight to Emily's body as their lips parted to allow their tongues to explore the uncharted territory of one another's mouths.

"Anika," Emily gasped, barely a whisper between parted lips.

"Emily," Emily felt Anika's reply on her lips as she slid her hand down the front of Anika's t-shirt. Anika's skin was uninterrupted and Emily felt the soft curves of her breasts through the thin cotton. Anika groaned at the gentle caress of Emily's hand over her breasts.

Anika pulled Emily closer, kissing her deeply, less tentatively. Emily kissed her back with a need that she had been unable to express for too long. Emily's hands found the hem of Anika's t-shirt. Anika's belly was warm, her skin soft under Emily's gentle touch. Emily let out a sigh of contentment at the feel of Anika. Anika moaned throatily as Emily ran her hand up and gently cupped her breast which was soft and supple, round and just enough to fill her hand.

She found Anika's nipple with her thumb. It stiffened in response to her touch and Emily gently squeezed Anika's erect nipple between her thumb and forefinger, still cupping her breast. Anika broke from their kiss and tilted her head back, hands on Emily's shoulders.

Anika brought her head down to meet Emily's eyes, with the same hunger Emily was feeling. Anika ran her fingers down Emily's back finding the hem of her t-shirt and pulled it upwards. Emily released Anika's breast and lifted her arms above her head to allow Anika to pull off her shirt. Emily's fine blond hair fell around her face as Anika discarded her t-shirt. Emily reached for Anika's t-shirt and pulled it over her head, her thick, red hair draping across her shoulders and over the soft skin of the swell of her breasts.

Both women sat up on their knees, just inches apart, looking intently into each other's eyes. Naked, blushed skin almost touching, radiated heat. The cool summer breeze coming through the window sent shivers through their bodies, adding to their sensations. Anika reached out and allowed her fingers to trace a gentle line along Emily's collar bone, down her chest to her ample breasts. Emily cried out at the caress of Anika's fingers over her erect nipples, which hardened further at the touch.

Emily reached to touch Anika's arm, fingertips barely grazing her smooth, freckled skin. Not wanting to break eye contact, but wanting to feel their bodies pressed together, they embrace. Their lips met and parted once again, exploring curiously. They both moaned in pleasure as their arms wrapped around each other and they took in the sensation of their breasts being pressed against each other; warm skin to warm skin.

"Anika," Emily whispered into her neck, relishing the soft skin of her back and taking in her scent.

"Emily," Anika whispered back, kissing the side of Emily's mouth and trailing a line of kisses down her jaw and neck. Taking Emily's generous breast in her hand, she cupped it, gently ran her thumb over her nipple. Bringing her head down to meet Emily's breast with her mouth, Anika gently sucked on her nipple then took more of Emily's breast in her mouth.

Emily moaned, running her hands up Anika's back and through her hair, pulling her closer. Anika kissed her chest and took the other nipple in her mouth, repeating the slow suckling on this nipple as well. Emily kissed Anika's hair and pulled her up to kiss her mouth passionately as she gently tugged on Anika's hair, her fingers exploring its curls.

Anika allowed her hand to wander down to the elastic of the pajama pants Emily was wearing, slipping her fingers between the elastic and Emily's stomach, caressing her waist. Emily mirrored Anika's movements and ran her fingers under the waistband of her shorts, as she pressed Anika's hip to hers.

Anika slid Emily's pants down over hips and Emily stood, allowing them to fall. Emily reached for Anika, pulling her up to meet her and slipped her hands down her hips and pushed Anika's shorts down. In the glow of the moon light, the women embraced, kissing deeply, their naked bodies together. What started as a slow ache, was now a burning fire.

Emily ran her hands down Anika's back as Anika kissed her neck. Emily's hands traveled down to the small of Anika's back and to the firm roundness of her generous bum, to which she gave a small squeeze, forcing a gasp of surprise, and a smile, from Anika's lips. Emily's hands slowly found their way around to the front of Anika's hips over the scars left from the children Anika had given life to. Emily trailed her fingers lower, to which Anika widened her stance slightly, allowing Emily's fingers access.

Both women panted heavily, expectantly. Emily took advantage of Anika's widened legs and slipped her fingers between Anika's folds and gasped in appreciation at the wetness. She moved her fingers in slow circles over Anika's clitoris, causing Anika to cry out in pleasure. Anika gripped Emily's shoulders as Emily slid a finger inside her. Anika cried out again and tightened her grasp on Emily's shoulders, causing her to pant as she continued to move her fingers in and out of Anika slowly.

Anika's hands searched eagerly over Emily's body; over wide hips that happily housed her two children.

Making their way over warm skin, pausing at Emily's clitoris for but a moment, Anika slid her fingers inside of Emily causing her to cry out loudly at the sensation as her body shuddered in response.

"Shhh," Anika smiled as she whispered and brought a finger to Emily's lips.

"Sorry," Emily giggled, her eyes closed.

Still standing, Anika removed her fingers and gently pushed Emily down onto the couch. Emily's skin was flushed and warm from arousal but continued to blush further as Anika pressed her body to hers forcing Emily down on her back. The leather was cool against her skin. Emily shivered from both the coolness of the couch and her arousal. She shyly brought her arms up to cover her breasts. Anika, leaning over with one hand on top of the couch, supporting her weight, looked down on Emily. Surprise and relief flooded Emily's senses at seeing the arousal and passion she was feeling reflected in Anika's eyes.

Anika lifted one leg from the floor and wedged it between Emily's closed legs, spreading them so she could lay between. Emily released her arms from her own chest and brought her hands to Anika's breasts cupping both gently, feeling her soft skin. As Anika leaned closer and lay on top of Emily, placing her elbows on either side of her head, she caressed her hair and brushed her lips across Emily's. Emily instinctively pushed up with her groin, causing both women to moan at the sudden sensation of their naked bodies pressing together.

"Am I too heavy?" Anika asked in Emily's ear as she gently nibbled and licked her earlobe, sending shivers through Emily's body. The first coherent words either woman had said in quite a while.

"No." Emily barely formed the word as Anika pressed her hips into Emily's and their lips met again, their tongues hungrily searching parted lips. They pressed against each other, rotating their hips slowly, when Anika sat up suddenly, sliding her body down on the couch.

Emily sat up and the women embraced. Emily kissed and bit Anika's neck, then brought her round breast to her mouth once again. She tried to gently push Anika down, bringing her lips lower on her chest and then to her stomach. Anika firmly brought Emily back up just as her lips grazed her hip.

"I want you first," Anika whispered into Emily's ear, nibbling on her lobe as the words escaped her mouth.

Emily flushed and slowly, somewhat reluctantly, laid back down on the cool leather, keeping Anika's head buried in her neck. Anika kisses moved down Emily's jaw, then her neck. She paused at Emily's breasts and appreciatively licked each nipple, savouring them. Gently using her teeth, she tugged on one of Emily's nipples, sending a warm sensation over Emily's chest. Anika trailed kisses down Emily's soft belly, circling her belly button with her tongue and nibbling Emily's hip.

"Anika!" Emily managed, surprised, as Anika slid

further down and kissed the inside of her thigh. Emily shyly spread her legs wider and Anika tentatively licked her. Emily gasped at the sensation of Anika's tongue on her.

Anika licked her again, this time taking Emily's inner folds in her mouth and gently sucking. Emily arched her back in pleasure and moaned as Anika pressed her tongue against her clitoris. Anika enthusiastically sucked and licked Emily, pushing her tongue inside Emily's wetness. Emily had never experienced such sensations; such eagerness from someone who wanted to show her pleasure.

Emily pulled Anika up to her and kissed her mouth deeply, tasting herself on Anika. The kiss deepened and Anika groaned deep in her throat. Sitting up, Emily pushed Anika gently onto her back with her legs open, panting heavily.

Emily slowly ran her fingers over Anika's jaw, over her breasts and down her belly to the soft, warm, arousal where Anika's open legs met. Emily slowly slid her fingers inside Anika, her wetness making entry effortless, as she leaned down to suckle Anika's nipple. She matched pace between her sucking and her fingers, watching Anika arch in pleasure. Flicking her tongue over Anika's nipples, she removed her fingers and slid down on the couch, kissing the inside of Anika's thigh, then further on, into her most sensitive area. Anika grabbed Emily's hair as Emily slid her tongue over Anika, lapping up her wetness. Both women moaned appreciatively. Emily flicked her tongue back and forth over Anika's clitoris, causing her to cry out in pleasure.

Anika pulled Emily up to kiss her. Tenderly their lips met briefly as they embraced, Emily burying her face in Anika's hair. Their bodies entwined, sitting on the couch, naked arms and legs wrapped comfortably around each other. Emily felt a sudden sense of curiosity and shyness with this woman in her arms.

"Ummm. Can I ask you a question?" Emily started, embarrassed at not knowing the answer to what was on her mind.

"Uh huh," came the alert yet muffled reply.

"Did you...." Emily trailed off, suddenly at a loss for words, not wanting to say out loud what she was thinking.

"No," Anika said quietly, anxiously. "Did you?"

"No." The women sat in silence.

"Can we have a shower? Together?" Emily inquired tentatively. Anika pulled apart from Emily, brushing the back of her hand across Emily's cheek and down her neck. Leaning forward, their lips brushed and pressed more firmly together.

"I'll start it and meet you there." Anika stood and walked in the direction of the bathroom. Emily watched Anika go and felt shy as she found her body responding again to her new lover as she crossed the room.

The shower was warm and full of sensation for the women as it massaged their aroused bodies. Silence encompassed the bathroom as both women replayed moments of the past hours.

"I'll wash your back?" Anika broke the silence, picking up a purple washcloth, holding it under the water to soak it. Putting the sweet-smelling shae butter body wash on the cloth filled the shower with warm scents, which added to their awakened senses.

"Ummm... Thanks," Emily replied, relishing in the feeling of Anika touching her again. Anika gently ran the wash cloth up and down Emily's back, over the curve of her generous hips and down her bum. Hanging up the wash cloth, Anika used her hands to rinse the soap from Emily's back, retracing the path her hand had earlier followed.

"I'll wash yours?" Emily inquired, picking up the wash cloth. Anika nodded and turned so her back was to Emily. Mimicking the trail that Anika used on her back, Emily washed down her shoulders and back, down her small hips and over her ample bottom. Emily rinsed Anika's back and, placing her hands on Anika's hips, she motioned for her to turn around. They embraced, closing their eyes to shield them from the water. The kiss was slow and full of expectation, carrying years of need. They continued to search each other's mouths; exploring, enjoying.

Anika had brought them each a robe, one black and one pale purple, for after their shower. As they finished drying themselves, Anika handed Emily the black robe which was thin and silky, soft on her sensitive skin. Anika put on the heavy pale purple terrycloth robe. They searched for and found each other's hands and Anika led

Emily out of the bathroom back to the couch. Emily could see that Anika was struggling with two choices: whether she should join Emily on the couch or kiss her good-night and go to her own bed alone. Emily lay down on the couch; half propped up, she opened her arms, motioning for Anika to join her. Anika lay down between Emily's legs, her head resting on Emily's chest. They fit perfectly together. Emily wrapped her arms around Anika and listened as her lover's breathing slowed.

I want to remember this forever, Emily thought to herself, as she relaxed and closed her eyes, her head settled on the back of the couch. She was tired, but did not want to miss a moment with Anika. Emily finally began to drift and her last thought, though it was more of a feeling than a thought, was of love.

CHAPTER 6

Emily awoke the next morning alone on the couch. She reached to pull the robe around her body. Sitting up and tucking her legs under her, she looked around for Anika. The house was quiet, but she could hear the girls giggling in Karianna's bedroom. She stretched and shivered, standing up just as Anika came into the living room from the direction of her bedroom.

"Hi," Emily said shyly, wrapping her arms around her body, hesitating where she was standing between the coffee table and couch.

"Good morning." Anika smiled, as if uncertain of Emily's reaction. A light breeze blew through the open window, fluttering the light curtains just as they had the night before. The breeze made both women's skin raise with goose bumps, a sensual reminder of the other's touch.

Emily sat down on the couch again and patted the seat beside her. The material was soft against her skin. "Sit with me?"

Anika nodded and sat close to Emily. Reaching her hand out, Anika splayed her fingers open in anticipation and expectation. Emily placed her hand in Anika's and they wrapped their fingers around each other's. Anika's hands were small and petite compared to Emily's. Although feminine, they were strong working hands. Emily stroked Anika's fingers with her other hand and stared at their fingers, intertwined. Anika reached up, stroking Emily's chin and gently turned Emily's face so they were looking into each other's eyes.

"Are you okay with last night?" Anika asked, vulnerably playing with Emily's wedding ring.

"Yes," Emily replied confidently. Closing her hand over Anika's, she settled the restless fingers firmly over her own hand. Then, asking hesitatingly and fearful of an admission of regret, "Are you okay with what happened last night?"

"I'm more than okay. Last night was..." Anika shook her head, searching for the words to describe their impassioned evening.

"Yes," Emily barely whispered, remembering how their lips felt together; remembering their most intimate moments. Emily leaned forward, as did Anika, and their lips met for the first time in daylight. Emily felt a release and sighed, sinking further into the kiss. She felt tears welling in her eyes and a rush of emotion. Their lips separated, though they remained touching, foreheads together. Anika ran her hand up Emily's neck and through her sweet-smelling hair and Emily grasped Anika's arm, feeling warm skin under her hand. The air stilled for a moment and both women could smell each other's bodies. The scent of warm, clothed, clean bodies ripe with desire filled them both and their breath quickened once again, just as it had last night.

The pitter patter of their children's feet broke the women apart. Emily got up and swept Julia, her youngest daughter, into her arms. "Did you have a good sleep?"

Julia nodded, her chubby face beaming, which reminded Emily of a child much younger than five. Claire wiggled in and hugged Emily's waist. Karianna, Dominic and Dedrick, Anika's children, climbed onto her on the couch, giggling and pushing each other for their mother's attention.

"I'm going to get dressed. We have to get home. I have a conference call in 45 minutes." Emily was a freelance editor, having to market and advertise herself to find work. This morning she had a call with a big company who potentially wanted her to edit for them exclusively. The position would give her the steady income she needed, but allow her the flexibility she desired as a mother, to care for and be an active part in her children's lives. She smiled warmly at Anika before she turned to go, who returned her smile. 'I love you' was on the tip of Emily's tongue and in her eyes. But she was unsure Anika felt the same and did not want to push her away, or rather, scare her away by being too needy. She wondered if the look she saw in Anika's earth-brown eyes reflected the emotion she was openly showing her own blue skies.

Emily felt a heat radiating up her spine as a flash of last night demanded her immediate attention, interrupting her thoughts of the day. Anika met her eyes with reflected hunger. Her cheeks reddened, but neither woman could break apart from the depths of each other's gaze.

"Mom. Mom, mom, mom, mom." Claire was tugging on Emily's elbow, but it took several moments for Emily to focus on the child.

"Yes!" she finally replied, unable to hide the frustration in her voice.

"Karianna won't let me pick my own socks." The women exchanged glances and Anika treaded down the hall to deal with the minor squabble that had been taking place much to the obliviousness of Emily and Anika.

Shaking her head to hopefully clear some of the fogginess left over from last night, and from the intense connection she had with Anika, Emily reached down and picked up the trucks and Barbies scattered at her feet. Making her way through the mess of doll furniture, dress-up clothes and puzzle pieces, she found the toy bins and started separating what she had in her arms. Arms empty, she continued to the bathroom.

Checking the time on her phone as she slid her shirt from last night over her head, Emily rushed to finish dressing and quickly ran a brush through her hair. *Shit! 15 minutes until my call.* She bit her bottom lip, took a deep breath to calm her nerves and hastily hung up the silky robe she had let fall to the tile floor.

"Come on girls!" Emily called down the hall. "We have to go!" As it always is with kids when parents are in a hurry, they were moving as slow as molasses. She ran her hands through her hair, giving her short lengths some temporary volume as she bent down to grab her purse from beside the door.

Emily looked up to find Anika staring at her through tired eyes, leaning against the doorway. Still in her robe, red hair messy and untamed, she reminded Emily of when she was above her looking down, lips parted and ready. Emily pulled Anika into an embrace. Feeling their bodies press against each other, they hugged tighter; neither woman wanting to let go. The women breathed in each other's scents: Emily burying her head in Anika's long, thick hair and Anika nestling in against Emily's neck.

"Thank you," Emily said softly, breaking away. Anika's hand lingered on Emily's hip as she stepped toward the door. Both women smiled. "I'll call you after my meeting, okay?"

"Not soon enough," Anika replied placing her hand in her pocket and leaning back against the door frame again.

"Oh! Wait!" Anika turned and ran down the hall through to the kitchen and came back a moment later holding a container. "I'd made these for us to share for breakfast, not thinking we'd sleep so late." Anika handed Emily homemade cheese and chive scones as well as chocolate scones.

"Thank you." Emily smiled, Anika's hand in hers,

and then, releasing her, walked out the door. The girls were already in the Subaru Forester ready to go, giggling as they tried to get their seatbelts secured. Emily paused with her hand on the door and smiled to herself. She had not felt this whole in a long time. She gave Julia a little tickle as she helped her tighten the seatbelt around her waist. Climbing into the driver's seat she looked back and smiled at her girls, feeling full of love.

The radio sang to them as she started the car and Emily laughed out loud at the lyrics as she backed out of the Anika's driveway: Katy Perry's, "I kissed a girl and I liked it…" Making a mental note to tell Anika, she headed for home.

CHAPTER 7

As she made herself a cup of tea, Emily was distracted by thoughts about the night before. It had come to each of them so naturally; not seeming weird or odd. Even though everything they did together was new, it felt like they had always been together. Blushing and unable to hold back a grin, Emily poured the boiling water over her minty tea bag. She relished the experiences she'd had with Anika, but was also concerned about the consequences on not only their friendship, but also on their marriages.

Emily picked up the phone and dialed Anika's number. Anxiously waiting for her to answer, she removed the tea bag from her favourite purple and blue striped mug and clumsily dropped it in the garbage can as Anika answered on the third ring. "Hello."

"Hi."

"Hi." The silence was thick and comfortable. Neither woman seemed to know where to start. Emily thought they should talk about last night: whether it would happen again, if either woman had regrets, whether their friendship was in jeopardy. Where would they go from here?

"How did your call go?" Anika asked, making the small talk–they both hated, although her tone was filled with genuine interest.

"It went well. They want to review my resume again and see another example of writing, as well as have me edit a document they will be sending me. After they've received this second round of my work, we'll have another call. If I get through this next series of interviews, I'll have the opportunity to work for them from home for six to nine months on a trial basis. If they like what I do, they promised me a full-time position. I'd have to move to the lower mainland, though."

"That's great news!"

"Yeah, I'm excited! Nervous too, and I hate the waiting. But it will all pay off in the end— hopefully." Emily could not help but smile, a reaction that reached not only her lips, but also her voice. Emily's lips were full and she rarely needed lipstick. Her teeth were not perfect, but when she was happy, the imperfection of her teeth went unnoticed. Her smile was contagious. It was the one feature that she could not fake, which often proved troublesome.

"I've been thinking a lot about last night," Anika began.

"Me too."

"Are you still okay?"

"I'm very okay. Are you? I…" Emily bit her lip,

pausing. She shifted on her feet as she stood in her kitchen, staring at the sink and absentmindedly playing with the tap.

"I'm more than okay. Last night was something else. I've never experienced anything like that."

"Neither have I. It was amazing and sensual and passionate. It was perfect in so many ways."

"I was worried that you wouldn't feel that way today, that you might have regrets. We'd both had a lot to drink…" Anika trailed off, letting the silence settle between them again.

"I don't regret what we did at all!" Emily replied vehemently. "Do you?"

"Not at all! I didn't want you to think I'd taken advantage of you."

"You didn't! I wasn't that drunk. I wanted to do everything. I was worried about you. I don't want to lose you as a friend. Your friendship means so much to me." Emily spoke with emotion. Anika was always there for her when she needed support, but Emily was fearful that acting on their primal desires may have affected their friendship. She sighed heavily and closed her eyes, her back firm against the fridge. Sex always seemed to change relationships for the worst, in her experience.

"Your friendship means a great deal to me as well." Silence again. The sounds of their children drifted over the all but quiet line they shared.

"I want us to happen again," Emily whispered,

feeling defenseless and exposed. She had given herself to this woman in every way possible and now her heart was wide open and at the mercy of this strong and vulnerable woman.

"Me too." Excitement flushed through Emily's body, listening to the words she had hoped to hear. She felt herself blushing and becoming aroused at the thought of touching and caressing Anika again. She remembered how their lips had felt on one another's. Their hands searching and finding.

"Anika…"

"Emily…"

"Anika… I have something I want to say. I know it's probably too early. I don't want to push you away or for you do think I'm too needy, but I have to say it." Emily paused, the butterflies in her stomach making her feel sick. She took a deep breath, fighting back the fear of rejection. "You've been a great friend, so supportive and always offering a listening ear. Anika. I love you. You don't have to say it back, but I think… I know… I've cared for you, probably loved you for a long time. Long before last night happened. Sorry if this freaks you out or if this wasn't what you needed or wanted to hear, but I do."

"Emily, I wanted to tell you I loved you last night. I couldn't have shared last night with you, if I didn't. I thought a lot about that this morning and I know I loved you before last night. I haven't ever been this close to anyone, let anyone this far in. Thank you for saying it. I don't think I would have. Not for a while, anyways."

"I wish we were together right now. I wish I could see your face." Emily sighed, sinking to the floor in her kitchen, watching the fan going around and around.

"Me too."

CHAPTER 8

"Will you have sex with my husband?" Anika gave Emily a sideways glance as she took a long drink from her Corona. November was still warm. The kids were in light sweaters and Anika and Emily could still sit comfortably outside. By this time each year there had been at least one snowfall, but the fall continued with unexpected warmth.

"I'm not sure," Emily said shyly, taken aback by the question and blushing as she digested it. She looked down at her hands, peeling the label off her almost empty beer.

They were sitting outside on the steps of Anika's backyard deck she had stained a deep brown, but the color appeared burgundy in the late afternoon light. Their five children played in the yellow and orange piles of leaves the maple trees had dropped. The last of the day's sun shone through the trees, preparing to set behind the hills. Unlike Emily's deck, which showed grey under the peeling beige paint, Anika and Matisse's was smooth and inviting; the renovations they had started at the beginning of the summer were finally completed in the last weeks of October. Emily could not help but think of the things she had hoped to complete with Conrad over the summer. He had promised they would tackle their growing list, such as repainting the shutters, cleaning and repairing the gutters and refinishing their patio. Once again, Emily's wishes were pushed to the side and whatever Conrad wanted to do took precedence.

"I haven't told Matisse about us yet," Anika continued, not waiting for Emily to expand on her short answer. Emily and Anika had been discovering and devouring each other for several months now and Emily knew that this conversation would come up eventually.

Emily raised an eyebrow at Anika. Although they had spoken about the need to tell Matisse about their relationship, Emily was not looking forward to what might become awkward dinners with both families or at least for the two women. As she fidgeted, she could feel the smoothness of the deck under her feet.

"He keeps asking questions about you. And I have told him some of what we talk about. About you. About us. That you may be interested in a threesome. That you weren't offended when I mentioned that we had considered you in that way." Anika took another long swallow of her beer while Emily sat down. She was still shy to this kind of talk, though her reticence stemmed from more than just embarrassment with her desire for Anika. She wanted to pleasure Anika, to have her to herself. She felt a deep yearning, one which, despite the control she was able to exert over the rest of her feelings, she could not tame.

"You will have to tell him eventually," Emily replied looking up from under her long lashes. Blushing, she continued, stammering, "I'm not sure about... umm... being with your husband though. It's different than us being together."

"We won't be able to be together any longer then," Anika stated matter-of-factly. She could be brisk at the best of times and was not always concerned about how someone else would feel when she spoke her mind. Emily was easily caught off guard by Anika's brusque responses. Though Anika had told her she was not a mean-hearted person, her short retorts could still be brutal.

Emily felt the rush of ideas that started to stream through her head. She thought of the first time she and Anika had been together, she thought of what it would be like to be with both Anika and Matisse, she thought of her husband and her marriage and she thought of how angry it made her that Anika could be so black and white when it came to such a complicated decision.

"I'm sorry that seemed insensitive," Anika continued, reassuring Emily in her way. "I just meant..." She let the sentence hang unfinished.

Emily remained silent but observed Anika sneaking a glance at her from the corner of her eye, trying not to make it obvious that she was trying so hard to decipher how Emily was feeling about the situation. Emily was complicated and Anika sometimes had trouble reading her. The flip side was that Emily had the uncanny ability to know what Anika was feeling, sometimes even before Anika realized it herself. Both women were trying to gauge where the other stood on the subject. Would Emily say yes? Was Emily willing to share herself with Anika's husband? Anika was asking a lot. In the short time they had been together, Anika had expressed her uncharacteristic reaction to wanting and needing Emily; Anika despised the vulnerability of those feelings. She did not need anyone, or so she said.

"Mom!" Dedrick, one of Anika's sons, interrupted. He was learning to use the potty and was calling for her assistance. Anika flashed Emily an apologetic smile, swung her beer up to swallow the last dregs and left it on the patio table along with the other empties.

"What are you thinking?" Anika asked, putting her arm around Emily gently, startling her from her thoughts. "This is for Matisse, for our relationship, for our marriage."

Anika was kidding herself by trying to convince either one of them that she was only doing this for Matisse. It hurt Emily to hear it, though; to hear Anika try to justify their feelings for one another. Both women had discovered a new awakening when with each other. Emily knew that the love that was missing from her life had also been missing from Anika's.

When Emily did not immediately respond, she continued, "I didn't mean to sound so abrupt. Being with you is exciting and I love it. I love you. But this path. This us. It started with my intention to... Well... I've fulfilled every other fantasy of his and this is the last one on his list. Also, I don't want to cheat on my husband."

Emily saw Anika's cheeks begin to glow as they spoke of fantasies. She grabbed Anika's hand, pulling her into the kitchen from the sun deck to start on dinner. As she did so, she could feel Anika's eyes on her, appreciating Emily's body. Anika loved Emily's body; Emily knew this by how often Anika touched her and wanted to be near her, how she reached for her when they were together. The womanly curves her clothing accented were part of her appeal. She may not have been thin by magazine standards, but she wore her curves with confidence.

Anika gave Emily's bum an appreciative smack when they were alone; an act that Anika had called very 'guyish', but Emily had reassured her it was not. Emily laughed and ran ahead to the kitchen. She took out the dinner ingredients and began chopping the salad vegetables.

"I'm thinking that...." Emily struggled to find a path through her tangle of emotions and thoughts. Her eyes were bright. Gorgeous blue eyes that were going to sparkle until the day she died, so full of wisdom beyond her years and kindness, more kindness than most deserved from her. She put down the knife she was using and wrapped her arms around Anika. They relaxed into the embrace. Emily instantly felt herself letting go of the stress of the conversation and she allowed herself to enjoy the fact Anika could do that for her. "I'm thinking that I would like to give the three of us a try, but have reservations."

Anika opened her mouth to say something but nothing came out. A nervous smiled played on her lips and she stared at Emily. Her deep brown eyes searched the sparkling blue ones just inches away.

"We need to do some planning and keep our lines of communication open if we're going to commit to this. I don't want to jeopardize our friendship for the sake of sex, no matter who it's for. You need to make sure this is something you also want. It's one thing for us to be together, it's another for you to see your husband with another woman." Emily explained in one long breath, leaning back against the cupboard, her arms crossed protectively across her chest. Her eyes turned away from Anika to the window, looking out into the backyard where their children were played happily in the sandbox. Her stomach was doing flips. "Don't throw sand, Claire!" She moved to the window and yelled at her daughter.

"I agree. I have the same concerns. However, I don't want Matisse to know it is planned. I want him to think it is spontaneous. I want us to still be okay after this. That is paramount for me. Our friendship." Anika came around the counter and embraced Emily. Emily buried her face in Anika's sweet-smelling hair and closed her eyes for a brief moment, wondering what life would bring her next.

CHAPTER 9

Emily was excited to take Anika for her birthday surprise. She could not wait to see the look on her face when they arrived at the jazz bar Anika had been talking about for the past six months. Emily had gone to great pains to keep the evening a secret from her so she had no idea where they were going. Both women looked forward to an evening away from their children. An intimate evening together. More often than not, they found themselves frustrated with the chaos that came with having five kids under the age of seven.

"You look great!" Emily exclaimed as Anika walked through the doorway to the kitchen wearing a thigh-length, high-waist black skirt and a white sleeveless top. With just a hint of makeup (far more than she wore on any typical day), she had added white and black heels that completed her outfit. Emily was fascinated by her allure, wanting to bring Anika close and kiss her; to tell her how beautiful she was. With their husbands nearby, she could not express what she felt, nor could she show Anika with her actions. Instead, she cocked her head to one side and smiled, raising one eyebrow. Slowly, sultrily, she licked her bottom lip and adjusted her blouse, exposing more of her ample breasts.

"So do you! I love your skirt," Anika returned, taking in Emily's body with obvious appreciation. Emily was wearing a knee-length purple and grey skirt with a matching purple blouse that accented her curves. The open buttons on her blouse showed a hint of the round swell of her breasts beneath the fine material. Emily caught Anika's attempt to stifle the lust suddenly apparent on her face. "Where are we going?" she asked.

"I can't tell you, silly. It's a surprise!" Emily emphasized the word 'surprise' in a mocking tone and stuck her tongue out at Anika.

"Don't be sticking that out unless you promise to use it?" Anika whispered.

"Oh, I usually follow through on those promises." Emily winked and, grabbing her purse from the table, she called, "Claire! Julia! I'm leaving!"

Both of her girls came running down the stairs from their bedroom, Karianna, Dedrick and Dominic close in tow. Matisse and Conrad were in the living room watching the hockey game and drinking beer.

"Be good for Daddy, okay?" Emily asked, kissing each of her girls, their little arms wrapped around her legs. "I love you."

"You guys, too. Love you," Anika echoed, kissing her kids and sending them off to play again. Walking to the living room, she bent down and gave Matisse a peck on the lips. His hand instinctively went to her bum and gave it a squeeze.

"Have fun," Matisse said distractedly, his eyes still on the game.

"Bye, Conrad. See ya, Matisse," Emily called from the doorway.

"Have fun, ladies." Conrad tipped his beer to them.

"Make sure the kids don't go to bed too late, please," Emily requested as she left the room. The women's heels clicked on the damp pavement over to where Emily's car sat parked. As Emily backed out of the driveway, Anika's hand found hers. Smiling, Emily turned the music up. John Legend sang, "You're my end and my beginning. Even when I lose I'm winning…"

"I love you," Emily said when the song was done.

"I love you, too, Emily," Anika replied. They sat in silence, enjoying the drive. Then Anika asked, "Where are we going? Please tell me."

Emily glanced over at Anika, trying not to give it away. Emily laughed and squeezed Anika's bare thigh.

"Well…," She began, hoping to stir up a bit more suspense. "There is this place. Overlooking the lake. Not too far from here…"

"Emily, there are lots of places overlooking lakes not too far from here. I can only assume we aren't going for a hike dressed like this." She run her hand up Emily's skirt, stopping just short of the warm folds where her thighs met.

Emily sucked in a breath as her pulse quickened and she found herself growing moist. Giving Anika a hard look, she turned her attention back to the road.

"You know that jazz bar you've been talking about?"

"Emily! You didn't!"

"I reserved a table for us, and a local band will be playing tonight. I think you'll like it. They have fantastic reviews."

"Emily—"

"And, you're not paying for anything tonight," Emily interrupted "It's on me. Happy Birthday, sweetie."

"Thank you, beautiful. Thank you," Anika said. Emily could see Anika wanted to argue about paying tonight, but besides a sideways glance of disapproval, Anika voiced no other objections. Emily wanted Anika to be happy and this was something she would not have done for herself. It was also something Matisse had no interest in.

"You're welcome." The women sat listening to the music. Neither felt they had to fill every quiet moment; they took solace in the times they were able to be silent together.

Emily pulled into the jazz bar. Parking at the far end of the parking lot, Emily shut the car off. Unbuckling her seatbelt, she turned to Anika and placed her hand on the back of her neck, playing with her hair. Leaning forward, Anika brushed her lips against Emily's. Emily returned the kiss, tightening her hand on

Anika's neck. Leaning forehead to forehead they sat listening to the sounds outside the car. As the reality of the parking lot and the world outside pulled them apart, they exited the car.

"Ready?" Emily asked with mischievousness in her voice, grinning at Anika.

"Ready," Anika replied, brushing the back of her hand along Emily's jaw.

Walking through the parking lot, Anika slightly behind Emily, Emily wished they could go hand in hand, proud and open about the love they shared. Instead, they were going as friends, compelled to hide who they were from the rest of the diners who had come to listen to the soulful music.

"We have reservations for two. Last name, Eckhart." Emily paused just inside the door where the hostess was stationed. The aroma of garlic and fresh baked bread wafted to them. The air had finally cooled outside and the summer had slipped to late autumn. Crisp air and coloured leaves announced the fall season. Anika smiled with excitement and appreciation at Emily as they waited for their table. Emily returned the smile and gave Anika's elbow a little squeeze, running her fingers down the back of her arm.

"Right this way." The hostess led them through the restaurant to a small table next to a window overlooking the lake where the sun was on its way down. They took their seats and gave their attention to the view outside and the décor of the restaurant. Simple yet classy, the burgundy tablecloths and walls complemented the rustic wood furniture, lending the room a warm intimacy. The band equipment was set up two tables away. "Your waitress will be with your shortly."

"Thank you," Emily replied, settling in and reaching for the drink menu.

"This is beautiful, Emily. Thank you." Anika spoke with feeling, her voice low.

"You're very welcome." Emily smiled warmly, once again wishing she could grab Anika's hand and kiss her. "Should we share a bottle of wine?"

"That sounds great."

"How about the Grey Monk, Gewurztraminer?"

"Are you sure that's what you want? We can order something else, if you'd like?" Anika asked.

"I'm very sure," Emily assured her, as their waitress approached.

"Can I start you off with drinks?" The waitress asked.

Emily ordered the bottle of wine. She played absently with her necklace, gently caressing her collarbone as she twirled her pearls around her fingers.

"Excellent choice! I'll be back in a moment with the wine while you look over the menus."

"Thank you," Emily responded, then, turning to Anika, asked, "What looks good to you? Do you want to share an appy?"

"I'd like that. How about the chili garlic prawns?"

"Yumm." Emily licked her lips, giving Anika a sultry look as she took a sip of her water.

Anika let out a throaty groan as she opened her menu, as if to push the desire to the back of her mind. "Anything look good to you? What are you ordering?"

"I think I'll have the filet mignon with the seasonal vegetables and mashed potatoes and gravy. How about you?" It was not food Emily was hungry for right now.

"The ribs sound good to me. I'll probably get rice, though, not potatoes." Their waitress appeared with their bottle of wine and glasses a moment later and took their order. The women sipped the sweet, crispness of the pale liquid in their glasses and looked over the water. Sitting high above the lake, they could view its full expanse.

"I love you." Anika's eyes had darkened and become serious. "More than I should. More than is fair."

"Anika. I love you. Very much."

"I'm very much enjoying our time together. I don't want it to end."

"Anika, it isn't going to end any time soon. I'm not moving anywhere right now. Things are good," Emily said, her eyes on Anika.

"I know, but at some point you'll grow tired of this. You'll want something else."

"I'm not interested in any other relationships. I think the one I have with Conrad, the one I have with you and the potential for one with Matisse is MORE than enough in my life." Emily laughed and took a large gulp of her wine.

"I know. But one day, when you aren't with Conrad, you'll find someone else. I don't want to share you. As it is, the thought of sharing you with my husband is already becoming a difficult. If you do find someone, what we have will be over."

"Anika…" Emily trailed off, pensive.

"To be honest, Emily, I would go on living like this forever, if I could. I would keep my relationship with my husband as well as build my relationship with you." This was not shocking to Emily. She'd had her suspicions that Anika felt this way for a long time now.

"You're right, Anika. In the perfect world, this would be the ideal way to live our lives, but unfortunately, my marriage is failing. I won't stay with Conrad for the rest of my life. And I had my suspicions that you didn't want to share me. If I end my marriage, having you only part of the time won't be enough for me. I want you, all of you. I don't want to share you with your husband either. I know you won't leave Matisse, despite our jokes about living together. You love him; you want the best for him and your children. Please don't trivialize your feelings for him or your need for a normal family. I get it. I really do. I just don't think I was made for normal. I want you to be happy," Emily said, allowing the sorrow of this disclosure to enter her voice.

"I want you to be happy as well. I fear that I don't make you happy at times. I don't want to hold you back from finding someone who will."

"Oh, Anika! You do make me happy. You support me and help me and calm me. You do so much for me!" Emily reached for Anika's hand and gave it a squeeze before releasing it. Smiling, she dropped her hand to her lap.

"Thank you, beautiful, for being you."

"Always."

CHAPTER 10

Emily's heart pounded as she dared to ask, dared to push Anika any further. She could feel her body responding, her feminine regions becoming tighter with the warmth of Anika's breath on Emily's neck. The heat of their bodies on the grey leather couch filled the room with the scent of passion and yearning. Emily squirmed involuntarily beneath the weight of Anika. They had come back from the jazz club and decided to stop at Anika's before returning to Emily's, where their husbands and children were sleeping for the night. Their evening together had been amazing and intimate, the music fantastic. They'd had good conversation, but some of it had been dark. Anika had allowed herself to indulge in a number of glasses of wine, since Emily insisted on driving them home. Both women were feeling the effects Anika's indulgence.

"Why don't you? Why can't you lose control?" Emily whispered into Anika's hair, smelling the sweet musk of her perfume as the scents of their bodies mingled into one arousing aroma.

"I can't. I don't want to hurt you. I have trouble

controlling myself when I'm with you. I don't want to ruin what we have." Anika's voice was hoarse. The night had required a forced self-control for both women. The music and atmosphere had acted as prolonged foreplay and now they were ready and wanting of each other.

"I want you to lose control. Stop thinking I can't handle it." Emily met Anika's lips and pressed her tongue between them to meet Anika's. Anika grabbed Emily's wrists and pushed her down on the couch roughly. Emily sucked in air with anticipation, briefly closing her eyes and allowing herself to feel Anika's grip on her wrists and the resistance on her arms from being pinned.

"This is okay then! Is it? Do you like this?" Anika spoke gruffly and leaned down, biting Emily's shoulder. Pain fanned down her arm and across her chest. "I want to have you. I want to leave my mark on you." Anika kissed Emily but this time bit her lip, then her jaw. Emily's breathing became shallow and quick. She could feel her wetness between her legs and she squirmed wanting Anika to touch her again.

Just as quickly as Anika had started, she sat up and released Emily. Emily had no words; she felt that she had seen a side of Anika that she had not yet experienced. It both scared and excited Emily. Anika watched Emily, combing back her thick red hair with her fingers. Emily's eyes revealed the passion and excitement she felt deep within her.

The silence was thick; Emily reached for Anika's

neck and pushed her down on the couch to kiss her. Their lips met and at once their hands were caressing each other's bodies. Hands ran up and down each other's hips, cupping curves and groping for more. Emily's hand found Anika's breast and she squeezed it gently, running her nipple between her fingers. Anika moaned in pleasure, arching her back and tipping her head back, giving Emily access to her neck. Emily pulled Anika's light-coloured nipple to her mouth and grazed her teeth along it, sensitive, erect. Taking it in her mouth, she sucked gently, causing Anika's ready body to arch again. Anika tugged Emily up to her lips to kiss her. Both women sighed in pleasure as their mouths explored and tasted the night's desire.

Emily brought her mouth to Anika's neck once more. She bit just under her ear and nibbled her earlobe. Anika let out a throaty groan and leaned her body harder into Emily. Emily kissed Anika, their mouths parting to allow their tongues access to each other.

The women were hot with arousal. Their skin warmed to the other's touch. Emily kissed, sucked and bit her way down Anika's body. The alcohol Anika had consumed let her fall easily into the pleasure that Emily wanted to give her. Emily brought her arms under Anika's legs and teasingly flicked her clit with her tongue, followed by a nip to her inner thigh. Anika let out short throaty moans of pleasure with each tease and nibble.

Emily found Anika's nipple with her hand and, as she dove deep into Anika with her tongue, Anika let out a cry. She gripped Emily's arm as Emily moved rhythmically with her mouth over the opening to Anika's vagina and her clit. Alternating between fast and slow, building to Anika's climax, Emily lapped up all that was Anika.

Releasing Anika's nipple, Emily adjusted her body so she could slide a finger inside Anika. Emily let out a groan at the ease in which she slid her finger. She could feel herself growing wetter the closer Anika came to her climax. Anika's lips were pursed tight together and her brow furrowed in concentration as she took in all the sensations.

Emily moved her finger in slow circles inside Anika while still licking her clit sending Anika over the edge. She tightened her hold on Emily's arm and pushed herself into Emily as she called out loudly in pleasure at her finale. Emily moaned while bringing Anika to her climax.

Wiping her mouth on the back of her hand, she gave Anika a kiss, slow and sensual when their lips met. Emily sank onto Anika's chest and listened while Anika's heart took it's time to slow as Anika basked in the glow of her release and the warmth of the woman in her arms.

Anika hugged Emily tighter then moved to position Emily under her. Anika gave Emily a mischievous grin, pecking her lips then trailing long slow kisses down her neck. Emily sighed as Anika's mouth found her nipple and she sucked. Emily tightened and felt herself growing wet again.

Anika's hands ran down Emily's hips and her mouth followed. Emily's body was hot to the touch, sensitive and aroused with expectation. Kissing Emily's folds, she used her hands to open her up and gain access to Emily's clit. She smiled appreciatively at the sight before her, making Emily blush further.

Anika slid two fingers into Emily. Emily let out a long feminine moan and swirled her hips to take Anika's fingers deeper. Pulsing in and out, Emily's body flushed as she crept closer to her climax. Emily sighed as Anika removed her fingers, but closed her eyes when Anika lay down to take all of Emily in her mouth. Sucking gently and using her tongue on Emily's clit, Emily reached for Anika's hair and took a handful to hold firm. Pulling Anika's hair brought Anika to quicken the pace of her tongue.

"Put your fingers back in me," Emily breathed, heavily, eyes closed, mouth partway open. Anika did not reply in coherent words, but obeyed and put a finger back in Emily, matching pace with her tongue.

Emily tightened around Anika's finger and her release came in throbbing pulses of gratification. Emily was loud, screaming in pleasure and arching her back to drive Anika's finger deeper. When Emily's orgasm had subsided, she pulled Anika up to her.

Anika laid on Emily's chest, pulling a blanket from the back of the couch over them. The women embraced there, listening to each other's breathing. Neither felt the need to put words to what their actions had expressed.

CHAPTER 11

"I don't have a drinking problem; I have a fucking asshole problem." Emily slammed the light maple-coloured cupboard shut as she and Anika were washing the dishes one evening. "I'm so fucking tired of him thinking that he can just do and say whatever he wants without any thought to what I want!"

"I'm sorry, sweetie," Anika murmured as she placed more dishes on the drying rack. "I think we have to talk about your overindulgence, though." Emily knew that Anika had her own demons with alcohol and that was probably why they drank so much when they were together. It was also why Emily knew she was going to have to tackle this burden, this family demon of her own, alone. It made her feel sad knowing that this was just one more thing pushing her and Anika apart. They were still very close and enjoyed the time they spent together. They had found comfort in each other's arms over the time they had shared. Everything from their children and husbands, to friends and extended family had brought them closer together. They worked well together as a team and found that they did more co-parenting together than they did with their husbands.

It was just the way it had always been for Emily, even in this relationship, always being the shoulder for someone to cry on; always being the supportive one. Throughout her life, she had always been the nurturer. She was always offering advice and helping everyone through difficult situations. She often found herself alone, though, and there were many nights when she cried herself to sleep.

That was part of the reason why she drank so much. She could loosen up, force someone else to take care of her. Someone always stepped up, but it was usually at the last second. Drinking allowed Emily to shirk the responsibility she felt to care for everyone else. She hated how it made her feel the next day: cheap and disgusted with herself. Each night of overindulgence brought back a lifetime of abandonment, neglect, loneliness and pain. The struggle between what she wanted and needed was the devil in her veins; drinking subdued the demons that drove her.

It was not hard for either of them to find offence in the normal offhand comment. Both Anika and Emily were particularly sensitive individuals. Both were intuitive and could read far too much into every word. Usually this was not a problem, but at times would result in unresolved conflict. They were always over-analyzing what the other one said, constantly thinking that each comment and glance meant more or less than it actually did. Anika liked to poke fun at what Emily considered serious matters. Sometimes Anika would see that Emily was too sensitive for her jokes, but other times she did not. Anika would often try to play both sides. When

ALL OF ME, ALL OF YOU

Anika, Emily and Conrad were together, Anika would engage with Conrad's abrasive humor, at the cost of Emily's feelings. Emily was not sure if Anika really thought her reactions were funny or if she was just putting on an act so Conrad did not suspect there was more to their relationship than met the eye.

"I can get carried away. I shouldn't drink as much as I do. I just don't know when enough is enough. I seem to lack the judgement piece that tells me to stop. Sometimes I just don't want to have to be in control any more. I can loosen up when I drink." Emily stared at the plate she was drying.

I love you for you. You need me to support you for a while. This is what I'm going to do. I will not take or want anything in return. That's all I have ever wanted to hear. Emily sighed, knowing that not everyone took from her willingly or even knowingly. All she wanted was someone to acknowledge the pain bottled up inside.

Anika often told her she did not want Emily to feel like she was being taken advantage of. It may not have been possible for anyone to convince Emily she was appreciated. Maybe it was impossible for her to feel loved. She often tried to imagine what it would be like to feel wanted, to feel like she came first, not second or third

"Just don't drink anymore. We don't always need alcohol when we're together," Anika said, noncommittally. She had said this before, but she was often the one refilling Emily's glass when empty.

"Thanks, Anika, but that's not fair to you either,"

Emily said, trying to sound sympathetic when it should be the other way around. Conrad's answer to Emily's concerns about her own drinking, which he brought up on many occasions, was that she could simply choose not drink. It was frustrating when no one seemed to understand that it was not that easy.

"We can have less. Conrad thinks that we drink too much when we're together. He has made a few references to us as lushes."

"What the hell does he know? He has no idea what our lives are like day in and day out. Constant battles with the kids, running the household as well as working full time. He gets to go to work and comes home and that is the end of it. He has no other responsibilities. He just does whatever he wants."

"I think that's most men in general."

"Probably," Emily agreed. "I hope I hear about the job soon."

"Me too! That is so exciting!"

"At least when I have confirmation one way or the other I can start to make plans."

"What do you mean?" Anika questioned. Emily had only told Anika some of what she was hoping for if she was given the position, and she considered telling her more as she played with the bowl in her hand while she dried it.

"Well, I'm tired of constantly fighting with Conrad. I'm tired of not being heard. I told him months ago that I wouldn't live like this any longer. I told him years ago that I was unhappy. If this job comes through, I might have the means to be financially independent. I won't have to live like this anymore."

"Emily..." Anika's lack of words showed her surprise at learning of Emily's life-changing decision. "Are you sure? Is that what you want? Are you ready to call it quits? Does it make sense to end it when you'll have such uncertainty in your life?"

"I'm done. I think I've been done for a long time, but the conversation we had a few months ago has solidified my decision. I won't keep living like this. It isn't fair to me or the girls, and in all reality, it isn't fair to him either for me to put on a fake front all the time. He clearly hasn't taken my unhappiness seriously because he's done nothing to change that."

"I know you're unhappy, Emily. I'm sorry. I want so badly for you to be happy."

"I know. Thank you." Emily embraced Anika. Anika ran her hand under Emily's shirt, giving both of them goose bumps at the skin-to-skin contact. Emily gently kissed Anika's lips, then her nose. It was rare for the women to show each other such open affection, but the kids were all playing downstairs in the playroom and neither of their husbands were home. "I'm worried about the girls, though. I don't want them to go without, like I did when I was a child. There is so much that I missed out on because my parents had no money, no motivation. I want them to have every opportunity in life; to have the ability to follow their dreams. Unfortunately, that means having money."

"I worry about you. I don't want you to call quits on something that might just need time. Men usually take longer to mature than women. I get it about the girls and wanting better for them. I struggle with that as well." Anika gave Emily a gentle smile.

"Conrad's had many opportunities to change, to grow and mature and he hasn't. He thinks his life is good, he doesn't need to do anything differently. I don't want to stifle myself or set that sort of example for my children, where I let him treat me as though I am just a passing thought, but I struggle with that. I want my kids to know how to be kind and considerate, but at the same time, I don't want them to watch my relationship thinking that it's normal and acceptable. I don't want them to let a man, or anyone for that matter, treat them the way their dad treats me, with such disrespect." Emily sighed, leaning closer and burying her nose in Anika's neck. "Besides, if I get this job I'm going to have to move and Conrad isn't going to be willing to go with me. He's happy here."

"I don't think Conrad realizes that you can make money at what you're doing. He thinks that because writing, editing, words in general aren't important to him. Because it isn't important to him, he doesn't see the value in it. He doesn't believe that anyone else sees the value either."

"This is a huge opportunity for me, it will launch my career as an editor. I will have more time with my kids, as well as be able to provide for us." Emily's body tingled with the excitement of the uncertainty of what was ahead. A move to the lower-mainland and a work-from-home position, save for the monthly meeting with her superiors, with all the flexibility she needed to raise her children. She would no longer have to bid on editing jobs or advertise her services. It was the freedom she had been dreaming of since she started down that path more than six years ago, before Claire was born.

"I'll miss you when you go. I know you'll get the job. You're smart, and you're perfect for it, too." Anika brought Emily close, in tears.

"Anika! I'm not going anywhere for a long while, even if they do hire me. I love you. I can see your brain working and hear you worrying. Please don't worry. I love you. I will always love you. We will figure something out together."

"I love you. Thank you. Thank you for loving me. Thank you for your reassurance."

"Always." Emily kissed Anika, slow and sensual. Both women savoured the taste of each other's lips. Anika's hand traveled over Emily's bum and their kiss deepened. "Besides, I thought you were coming with me?" Emily joked, pulling away and gazing into Anika's eyes teasingly, though searchingly.

Anika looked away; the silence suddenly felt heavy between them.

CHAPTER 12

Emily carefully scrutinized the contents of her closet. Tonight would be the night, the night that the three of them would end up being together. She bit her lip as her stomach flipped and she felt a little sick. She was unsure if her nerves were about admitting to herself that a threesome was a long time fantasy of her own, or due to the fact she was cheating on her husband and had very little remorse for it.

Emily never thought of herself as particularly beautiful; attractive, sure, but not a beauty, nothing out of the ordinary. Anika had a very different opinion of Emily. Anika said Emily's beauty was evident inside and out, something she never stopped craving. She said that part of Emily's appeal was that she had no idea how beautiful she really was. Emily would scoff at the remarks, brushing Anika off every time spoke like this. Men had always chased after her; there was always someone who wanted her, even after she married and had children, but she had never considered herself exceptional. She was just average, the same as everyone else, and in all actuality, her thoughts were that she was probably less than everyone else: less important, less needed, less wanted. Every time she started to think that she was pretty, she felt guilt. She did not deserve to be pretty, let alone beautiful. Her feelings of inadequacy stemmed from a childhood of abuse and an early adulthood of emotional neglect.

"Hey," Emily called as she came in the house with her kids, dodging the flailing arms and legs as they ran past her, screaming their welcome. Shaking her head to clear the negative thoughts lingering, Emily put on a smile as she entered Anika's kitchen.

"How are you?" Anika continued with her dinner preparations as she looked over at Emily. Sitting on the leather stool at the bar, the beige and grey marble felt cool on Emily's arms as she rested them casually, trying to relax. Anika was wearing a frilly apron patterned in different shades of pink. Although the apron was not out of character, the pink was. A close aunt had made it for her years ago as a wedding present and she loved it despite the gaudy colours. Under the apron her curves were covered by a pair of jeans that accented her supple bottom and a purple checkered top that clung to her breasts. Her thick red hair was down around her shoulders and her cheeks were flushed from the heat of cooking as well as the whiskey over ice in her hand. "Would you like a glass of wine?"

"Yes, please," Emily replied, blushing at the intense stare from Anika. Their nerves were getting the best of them with ideas of what the evening may hold. "I'm good. Kids were good. Managed to get my house somewhat in order."

ALL OF ME, ALL OF YOU

Anika smiled at Emily as she turned to the fridge to fetch the wine chilling there. "Do you mind grabbing a glass?" Anika asked with her back turned to her friend.

"No worries," Emily replied, getting up from her bar stool and heading over to the china cabinet where the wine glasses were stored. "Am I just grabbing one?"

"Three please." Anika's voice was soft and broke as she said the words. Emily felt them more than she heard them and her stomach and heart lurched at the implications of the simple phrase. The evening, and its potential, had now become real.

"Hey. How are you?" Matisse's voice interrupted Emily's thoughts as she was retrieving the wine glasses from the cabinet across the room.

"Oh!" Emily exclaimed, then chuckled, "You startled me. I'm doing well. The kids were a bit challenging today, but all ended up happily enough. How was your day?" Emily tried to avoid Matisse's eyes, but eventually had to meet them as she walked back to the bar with the three glasses. Emily opened her mouth to say something else, but bit her bottom lip instead, slipping by Matisse. Her perfume swirled around her in a warm scent, causing a reaction Emily could sense, his attraction to her reflected in his face.

"It was good." Matisse was not much of a talker. Anika knew this, but Emily was new to deciphering Matisse's moods.

"You must be happy to be home? Anika said you've been out of town for a couple weeks working on a big project." Emily stumbled on her words as she watched Anika pour their much-needed glasses of wine. She felt her cheeks flush under the gaze of both her lover and her lover's husband as he slipped onto a bar stool beside Emily, reaching for a glass of wine.

"Yeah." Matisse took a long swallow. Emily followed suit; the wine was cool and crisp between her lips, sweet. It was a Gewurztraminer, one of Anika's favourite. Both Emily and Matisse preferred red wine, but this white was not so bad. It suited their needs at the moment. Emily traced the pattern of the marble with her index finger.

* * * *

Anika, Matisse and Emily all sat on the grey leather couch. The kids were settled for the night in their rooms, the girls watching a movie in Karianna's room and Dedrick and Dominic sleeping in their bunk beds in their room down the hall from the girls. Matisse sat in the middle; all three kept their insecurities and nervousness hidden. The only indication was their rigid postures and the small amount of space between each of them. Emily could smell Matisse's cologne. It was musky and sweet; a mixture that made Emily squirm.

Matisse was an attractive man with dark skin. He tried to take care of himself and had strong arms with muscles visible and defined under his t-shirt. His most attractive feature, though, to Emily, was his eyes; they were dark and always seemed to be searching, seeking. Anika explained that it was a search of expectation that was always present; he felt the world owed him something.

He's not the guy you think he is, Emily remembers Anika telling her. *He can be very controlling. There are years of history to our relationship. He's unpredictable. You think I have a temper?* Emily thought back on all that Anika had told her about her husband and felt uneasy. But, when Matisse looked at her again, with those dark brown eyes that seemed to draw her in, the unease she felt, the unpredictability of the night, vanished. She felt almost helpless when he looked at her, the same helpless she felt when Anika looked at her. It was the same deep, appreciative stare that she had come to accept. Both of them were wanting and full of expectation tonight. Emily hoped she would not disappoint either one of her soon-to-be lovers.

Matisse placed his hand on Emily's thigh. They sat beside each other on the couch, awkwardly still. Emily had done her best to look comfortable but was still trying to keep some distance. She was nervous and impatient; feeling as though she felt more self-conscious than either Matisse or Anika must. Quiet music played in the background, The Goo Goo Dolls singing of life's meaning "And don't it make you sad to know that life is more than who we are."

Emily took a long sip of her wine as she heard the door to the girls' room open and their carefree childhood giggles escape. "I'll deal with that," Anika said, getting up and placing a firm hand on Emily's shoulder, making eye contact as she left.

"You're off until early next week now?" Emily

inquired, between sips of wine.

"Uh huh." Matisse nodded.

They sat together in an awkward silence. Emily was not sure what she should be doing, but Matisse made the first move, placing his hand on Emily's leg. Emily set her wine on the glass coffee table in front of her while Matisse caressed Emily's leg. Emily allowed her hand to rest on Matisse's and massaged his knuckles. The sensation sent shivers through her. Emily closed her eyes for a moment to take in his warm hand under hers, the music and the sound of his breathing, which had quickened. Emily opened her eyes to Matisse staring at her intensely with those dark, needy eyes.

Matisse placed his wine on the table beside Emily's and reached to take hold of her. Gently pulling her into him, their lips met for the first time. It had been nearly ten years since Emily had kissed a man other than her husband. It had been much longer than that since Matisse had kissed another woman. Emily's past experiences, from before she was married, easily out numbered the experience that either Matisse or Anika had. Matisse's lips were firm, but longing on her own. She noticed the difference between him and Anika. She wondered if it was due to the way men and women kissed, or just due to individuality. She also wondered which she preferred.

Emily's hand was still on top of Matisse's, which was now mid-thigh. Her other hand lay limply on the couch. Matisse's hand moved up Emily's neck to the back of her head and he entwined his fingers through her fine, short blond hair, which she had curled. Their lips separated and touched again. Emily felt her body rapidly responding to the sensations throbbing through her. She tried to restrain the urge to squirm under the increasing arousal she was feeling. She clutched Matisse's hand and parted her lips further meeting his tongue with hers and sighing unconsciously with a primal sense of pleasure. Out of the corner of her eye, Emily caught movement from the hallway and she broke away from Matisse. She saw Anika watching them, leaning against the wall. She was hard to read, but her flushed face and relaxed body language conveyed how turned on she was; how pleasing she found the act of watching her lover and her husband beginning to make love.

"Sorry," Emily said, reaching for her wine and pulling away from Matisse.

"No," Anika replied firmly, indicating her appreciation of their sensual interaction. "Please continue." Anika's voice is hoarse and throaty as she walked back to the couch, retrieving her wine and taking a long swallow.

"Are the kids settled?" Emily inquired, still blushing and wanting to make conversation. Emily felt guilty: her children were in a room down the hall and she was making advances on a woman and her husband. That guilt was quickly replaced by excitement and desire as she watched Anika's hand caress her own.

"Julia is sleeping, but Karianna and Claire are still awake. They should be asleep soon, since I took out the cat. And the movie just ended." Matisse's hand was still on Emily's thigh, gently running his fingers up and down her leg. Anika placed her hand on the back of his neck and kissed his ear lobe. Emily swallowed the last of the wine and placed the glass on the table with both hands, trying to calm her nerves.

Matisse turned to Anika and kissed her lips, his hand still on Emily. Emily placed her hand on top of his once again and she shifted closer, bringing her other arm up to the back of the couch to rest on Anika's. The grey leather couch protested her move, making Emily's heart jump; everything sounded, everything felt loud.

Emily moved her hand from on top of Matisse's to his thigh and he let out a small, surprised moan. Anika found Emily's hand and gave it a squeeze. Running her hand up Emily's arm to her neck, she pulled Emily closer so Emily and Matisse's heads were touching. Matisse turned from Anika to meet Emily's lips once more.

* * * *

Emily was stretched out on Anika and Matisse's bed, touching herself as she watched them kiss and fondle each other. The down comforter was covered by a yellow and blue duvet. The couple's spacious room was painted a pale grey and dimly lit by candles. Two oak high boys lined one wall with a full-length mirror in between. Large picture windows were covered by thick blue curtains and a curtain of the same colour opened to the walk-in closet. The room was warm, inviting; the place where Anika and Emily had shared many evenings together.

Anika poured her body across Matisse and kissed Emily's mouth with passion. One of each woman's breast in Matisse's hands and he gently played with their nipples. Emily returned the kiss, running her free hand through Anika's thick hair. Matisse's mouth on Anika's nipple made her moan with pleasure as Emily met his eyes. Anika motioned for Matisse to roll onto his back so she could climb on top. Anika sucked on Emily's sensitive nipple. Emily closed her eyes and concentrated on the feeling of her own hands on her body and listened to the sounds in the room as Anika mounted Matisse, hoping to climax soon.

"Come on!" Anika muttered, unhappily. Emily opened her eyes to see Anika struggling to coax Matisse into her. He had been hard a moment ago when he'd been touching Emily, but that was not the case now.

"Maybe I need a minute!" Matisse hit the oak headboard above Anika's head and roughly pushed her off. He walked limp and naked toward the door to go to the bathroom. Emily quit touching herself and reached for Anika, who was lying on the bed next to her.

"Are you okay?" Emily asked, searching Anika's face. Anika did not answer, but kissed Emily's red lips. The door to the bathroom slammed shut and the sound of water filtered through the shared wall.

"Anika, we don't have to do this. I can go get dressed. Go to the spare room—"

"Shhhh." Anika placed her finger on Emily's lips, which Emily kissed. "It'll be fine. We'll try again in a bit. For now, though, I have you all to myself." She smiled as she reached for Emily, but there was no smile in her eyes.

CHAPTER 13

Emily was between Anika and Matisse, which gave Anika a view of the sight unfolding in front of her. Emily's breasts were in Anika's mouth, who was appreciatively suckling her nipples. Matisse, who was trying very hard not to come, was rhythmically pounding into Emily from behind. Emily was a mass of sensation, though nowhere near coming yet. Emily had never experienced an orgasm with a man in her before. This was something that Anika had been hoping to remedy, as Matisse could be very patient and was so with Anika as it often took her a longer time to come.

Anika made eye contact with Matisse, but he misread her look and allowed himself his release. Disappointment flushed through both women and suddenly Emily felt embarrassed and exposed. Being sandwiched between the married couple, Anika clearly not happy about what had just happened, Emily wanted to disappear.

"Ummm..." Emily started, hoping to indicate to Matisse that he was going to have to move so she could go clean up.

"Matisse!" Anika said harshly, trying to reach for the Kleenex beside the bed.

"Sorry," He mumbled in a dazed voice. Anika handed the bunched-up Kleenex to Emily as Matisse got off the women and retreated to the bathroom. Emily got up from the bed and started to clean herself.

"I'm sorry. I was trying to tell him to keep going and he thought that meant finish. He thought you'd finished."

"That's okay." Emily avoided eye contact, feeling embarrassed and suddenly very aware of her nakedness. Anika was angry with Matisse. The night had not been going quite as they had planned, or had hoped. Emily threw the dirty tissues in the garbage can between the dressers, under the mirror.

"I'll be right back." Anika tossed a robe from the back of the door to Emily and grabbed one for herself as she opened the door of her bedroom. Emily heard Anika open the bathroom door down the hall and close it. The bedroom wall was adjoining the bathroom and despite her trying to ignore the voices on the other side of the wall, she could not help but over hear.

"I thought I told you not to stop." Anika's voice was calm, but Emily could sense the roiling emotion in her words.

"I thought you meant it was fine, she was done."

"Ummm. No."

"Sorry." There was silence. Emily found her bra

and panties she had discarded earlier and hastily put them on. She pulled the robe around her and tied it tight. Still feeling naked, she sat on the edge of the bed with her head between her hands. Several minutes passed when she heard muffled passion in the bathroom. Emily groaned, wishing her clothes were not in the very bathroom where Anika and Matisse were now engaging in sex play gone wrong.

"What the fuck, Matisse?" Anika's voice was loud and sounded frustrated through the too thin wall.

"Sorry, Anika," Matisse spat.

"Seriously?!" Anika's voice was getting louder.

"Sorry!" Matisse's annoyed voice carried through wall. Matisse said something else that Emily could not make out and then she heard the sound of running water. Emily shook her head, unsure what she should be doing. The bathroom door opened and slammed shut again. Emily stood up, expecting Anika to come into the bedroom, but the door never opened. Muffled footsteps made it to the front door and Emily heard the jangle of keys and then too-fast tires backing out of the driveway.

The bathroom door opened and closed and a moment later the bedroom door opened and Matisse stood there, clothed from the waist down. Emily blushed, wearing Anika's short purple robe and her undergarments from before. Matisse stood in the doorway, hands in the pockets of his black and grey pajama pants.

"Where did Anika go?"

"I dunno."

"Are you guys okay?"

"I'm sure we'll be fine. She's just pissed off. She'll get over it."

"I'm going to go get dressed. Excuse me." Emily tried to pass by Matisse without touching him but he took up most of the doorway, not moving. She could feel his warmth as she passed and she was aroused by his smell, despite willing herself not to be. She kept her eyes on the floor and turned the corner to the bathroom. Shutting the door behind her, she slid down and hung her head between her legs. She wanted to cry, but no tears came despite the emptiness and confusion she felt.

* * * *

Emily stayed in the bathroom as long as she could, but she finally had to come out. She had found some pajamas that Anika had left out for her in the bathroom and decided a shower was her next course of action. Allowing the warm water to fall around her body, she soaked up the muted sounds of the shower and tried not to think.

Wrapping Anika's housecoat around her clothed body, she made her way to the kitchen, hoping a cup of tea would help her make sense of the situation. Anika still was not back from where ever she had gone. Emily desperately wanted to talk to her; to make sure everything was okay between them. Emily thought she knew what the fight was about in the bathroom, but did not want to jump to conclusions. Her head swirled with the events of the evening and she suddenly was not so sure about her involvement with a married couple.

Finding the kettle and putting water on, she stood staring at the stove, lost in her thoughts, praying that Matisse stayed in his bedroom. She hoped she would not have to face him without Anika here. A hand on her shoulder startled her from her lost thoughts. "Oh!" She exclaimed, turning around to find Anika's brown eyes dark.

"Hi, beautiful. Sorry. I didn't mean to scare you." Anika's hand dropped from Emily back to its place at her side. Emily reached out and pulled her in, embracing her. Anika wrapped her arms around Emily tightly, breathing in deeply.

"Hi, sweetie. No worries. Are you okay? Are we okay? I'm sorry. Maybe we shouldn't have done this. Maybe we should have planned—"

"Emily, I'm not sure this was a good idea. I'm sorry. You have nothing to be sorry for. We're good. I just have a lot to think about. A lot going on in my head."

"I heard you guys arguing in the bathroom." Emily was consumed with worry for Anika as well as for their relationship.

"I thought I could go in there and get him pumped up and able to go again. I thought maybe we could have some fun, just the two of us in the bathroom, but he couldn't get it up. Usually he is ready to go right away, but apparently I wasn't doing it for him tonight."

"Anika…" Emily started, but faltered, uncertain of what to say.

"He didn't seem to care much."

"Anika, I'm sorry."

"Whatever. This won't ever happen again. Clearly it can't happen again."

"Did you talk to him?"

"I called him on my way home. He didn't have much to say. Not even a real apology. Hardly even a care for where I was or if I would return."

"I'm sorry." Emily busied herself making her tea, trying to find footing on this slippery slope. She gestured to Anika with the kettle and Anika shook her head, crossing her arms in front of her and leaning against the counter opposite the sink.

"That's okay. What's done is done. Might as well just move on with it. I'm sorry I dragged you into this."

"I was a willing participant. I wanted to have a little fun as well as help you to enhance your marriage. I'm sorry it hasn't turned out that way." Emily started to fear what this failure might mean for her and Anika. Would they continue their sexual relationship, or was what they had now over?

"I was thinking maybe we should try again, but I don't know!? Maybe when we've settled down. Maybe with more planning, we could take it slower. We did kind of jump into things quite quickly tonight," Anika rambled.

"Yeah, we should have taken it slower. I don't know if that would have made it any better, though. I don't think I'm willing to try again." Emily was blunt, not offering any further explanation for her decision.

"Matisse was such an asshole when I talked to him on the phone." Anika threw her hands in the air in defeat. Emily quit playing with her tea bag and went to Anika putting her hands around her waist, stepping wide around her legs. The women embraced, their bodies pressed tight together. Anika ran her hands up and down Emily's back over the robe she was wearing. They stood cheek to cheek for several minutes, listening to each other's breath. Taking in the sensations of their bodies together.

"I love you." Emily broke the silence. *If only it were that easy,* Emily thought to herself as they continued to stand in the dimly lit kitchen, the sounds of the warm weather drifting in through the screen of the open sliding glass door. Emily embraced Anika fully and tightly and once again repeated the words both women so desperately hear.

"I love you," Anika sighed, and she had no sooner said the words than Emily saw Matisse come around the corner into the kitchen. Emily pulled away in guilt. Anika turned to face Matisse standing in his pajama pants, and a plain black t-shirt. The look on his face revealed he'd heard at least part of the women's exchange.

"You love her?" he said out loud, not breaking eye contact with Anika.

"Matisse," Anika started, not answering his question, arms folded against her chest. He shook his head, turning and walking back in the direction he had come. "Shit," Anika whispered under her breath.

CHAPTER 14

The children seemed to be extra noisy and lacked the ability to follow even the simplest directions. Both Emily and Anika were losing their patience with the kids. Some of this impatience was caused by the stress of trying to put on a false front when their relationship was in turmoil. Since the threesome, Matisse had been keeping close watch on the women. Emily and Anika tried, with difficulty, to be nothing more than friends now; a task easier said than done. It was taking its toll on their relationship.

"Karianna! Come here!" Anika raised her voice, exasperation and frustration seeping into her words. "I have to get angry before anyone will listen to me!" Anika added, just as Karianna arrived.

"I've asked you again and again to stop leaving your shoes out. You've lost TV for the night now!"

"But Mom! That's not fair!" Karianna whined, jumping up and down as she came downstairs from Claire and Julia's room, where they were playing.

"You're seven! Quit acting like a baby! Jumping up

and down isn't going to get you your own way! Just go!"

"No!" Karianna defiantly crossed her arms and pouted, looking up at her mom through long eyelashes, red-blonde hair hanging in her face.

"Go! Before I get really angry!" Anika yelled at Karianna, pointing her finger up the stairs.

"Karianna, you have to be respectful. That's enough." Emily touched Anika's arm to calm her. Emily meant the touch to reassure Anika, to affirm her support.

"Fine!" Karianna yelled, stomping up the stairs as loud as she could.

"No one listens until I get angry!" Anika reiterated again, throwing her hands up placing them on the counter, pulling away from Emily in the process.

"You don't have to get angry," Emily told Anika,

"Thanks," Anika spat sarcastically, avoiding eye contact.

Emily felt tears welling in her eyes and fought to hold them back. She turned to busy herself at the stove. *I just want you to be happy. I thought I was helping. I'll back off. I'm sorry.*

She did not want Anika to see her on the verge of tears. Each time that happened, Anika shut down further. Emily's emotions often betrayed her by displaying exactly what she was feeling, whether it was by crying when she was upset, or becoming flushed when she was turned on.

Right now, though, Emily was feeling helpless. She

had tried on several occasions to talk to Anika about some of her anger issues. Each time she did, Anika shut down and refused to talk. Later, Emily would receive a text or an email from Anika, explaining herself; Anika needed to work through it, but any headway seemed nonexistent.

Emily concentrated on the music in the background. Rihanna sang, "...funny you're the broken one, but I'm the only one who needed savin'." The right song never failed to come on while they were having a fight.

"Anika," Emily pleaded with her back to Anika. She prayed she sounded calmer than she felt.

"No. Just don't. You don't get it. I don't need this with you too." She picked up her phone and started scrolling through Facebook. A distraction from the immediate triggers.

"Anika. I don't want to fight with you either. I'm not fighting with you."

"Then what do you call this? I don't need your constant criticism."

"That's not how I meant it. I'm not criticizing you."

"I don't want to fight with you. I don't want to talk about it." Anika would not meet Emily's eyes. The women stood across from each other in Emily's kitchen. The island between them as it always seemed to be.

"What are you thinking?" Emily asked Anika tentatively. The kids were noisily playing around them.

"I don't want to talk about this." Usually, Emily

and Anika were able to navigate their complicated relationship with the understanding they shared, but when their kids were involved, and the women were sensitive as they were now, they both put up a wall.

Emily often felt like she was not being listened to when it came to suggesting child-rearing practices. When Anika brushed her off, it was a trigger for Emily. It was so easy to lose patience with their children, who ranged in age from three to seven, but it was important to exercise reason when their children were out of control.

Emily had learned that children will push as far as they can if it means they can get a reaction. If the child knows the parent will not take action until they start to shout, then the child will wait until then to do what the parent has asked. If you act immediately at the first sign of disrespect or disobedience, the child will know that that they must comply with the parent or caregiver. Yelling never really works, even if it seems to bring the desired result.

Anika had unresolved issues with anger and shouted to make her children listen. Emily tried her best to be supportive, but the situations sometimes proved overwhelming, especially when Anika was not fair with the kids.

"I don't want to fight with you." Emily realized she was not being the friend that Anika needed. But she was still reeling from the sudden change in Anika. Her demeanor, her behaviour was hard to accept. Emily's intuition told her that the problem was not just the difference of opinion. She dreaded what might be coming. She briefly wondered if Anika had decided to call it quits on their relationship or if Matisse had discovered they were still lovers. He no longer approved of them being intimate after the failed threesome.

Anika nodded but did not respond further. She played with a piece of paper, rolling it around in her hands. Her lips were pressed tight together and her eyes were dark, hiding herself behind them.

"Anika, I don't want us to ignore what is going on. It's more than just a disagreement over the kids. It's not easy, but I don't want to sidestep this discussion. We both want this relationship to be perfect because there is so much in our lives that is far from that ideal. We'll never grow, if we ignore our issues; if we choose not to talk about them for fear of the pain. Please talk to me."

What else could Emily do but show her that she would be there for her no matter what? They had always said that their friendship was more important than anything in the world and they would not let anything separate them from that. The connection and feelings that they had for each other were not going to just vanish because they were not going to be sexual together any more. If anything, the less they had, the stronger the pull.

"I know that's what you think and I understand, but it's different with my kids, especially with Dedrick and Dominic. They're little boys and it's different when it isn't your kid. They only respond when I raise my voice. When Karianna acted up at the same age, I could sit down and reason with her. I have to get angry with them to make them listen." Anika stopped. Emily chewed on her cheek as she processed what Anika had said

Emily turned her back to Anika to put away the dishes. She did not want to make eye contact for fear of giving away to the negative thoughts she was having; how much she disagreed with Anika and how much she was tired of repeating herself. Anika often said that Emily was offended by the things that she said. This was not at all true. There were many times when Emily just had another opinion. Emily was the kind of person who took everything personally, but it did not mean she was offended. She just felt as though she should take responsibility for what was going on and the opinion being stated. Unfortunately, parenting is one of those things where most of the time no one has a clue if it is being done right. Oftentimes the results are not apparent until it is too late to do it differently.

"There's more going on here than just our disagreements, but that aside, I still need more support from you. Just a listening ear, not advice," she replied. Anika's dark eyes darkened even further. The threat of a tear built in the corner of Anika's eye and Emily felt the need, the want to reach out to catch it before it fell, but her pride stopped her. Anika held her voice steady by gripping the counter. "I want us to be easy..."

Emily closed the cupboard and stood staring at the maple doors she had always hated. She walked stiffly around the island, not wanting to breakdown, wanting to wrap her arms around Anika. As much as Emily did not agree with Anika's parenting style, she did not want to argue with her either. She was not giving into Anika, just postponing the inevitable.

Although Anika did not verbalize the obvious, Emily knew there was a delicate balance between their desire and the constraints placed on their relationship. Anika struggled with guilt, but could not bring herself to keep from engaging romantically. Both women felt an emotional, mental and physical pull and sometimes, there was no separating the three.

Anika wrapped her arms around Emily and leaned into her embrace, sighing. They listened to the meaningful words of the music playing, "What about the times you said to me, that I was everything you'd always need," Lady Antellebelm, singing of love.

"I want easy, too," Emily whispered in Anika's ear.

"I'm sorry I got so emotional. I have to remind myself that you aren't coming from a place of judgement," Anika replied, leaning closer. Her anger had finally run its course.

"Never am I coming from a place of judgement." Emily hugged Anika closer to her, feeling her arms tighten in response. Their bodies comfortably fitting together as though they were one. "There aren't ever any judgements from me. I'm sorry, sweetie. I'm sorry I'm not better at just having a listening ear sometimes."

"Don't be, beautiful. I'm a little sensitive right now." They stood in silence. "You know… I'm kind of jealous of Conrad."

"You have nothing to be jealous of Conrad. He only

occupies physical space in my life. He chose a long time ago to have no part of me." Emily scoffed at the thought of him, dismissing him with a wave of her hand and wrinkling her brow in disapproval.

"You know he doesn't see it like that, right?"

"I don't understand that way of thinking. It makes no sense."

"He believes he's doing a good job as a husband and a father. He works and all the bills get paid. To him that's all that matters."

"It certainly seems to be that is the way he feels." Emily's eyes welled with tears of sadness and failure. She took a deep breath, closing her eyes, she let the tears recede back into her eyes. Feeling the painful tears slide down the back of her throat as she swallowed hard, she gripped the edge of the counter to give her a sense of control.

"Honey." Anika placed her hand on top of Emily's to release it from the counter. Pulling Emily into her, they wrapped their arms around each other again. "I'm jealous that he gets wake up beside you. I'm jealous that he goes to sleep beside you each night. I'm jealous that he gets to occupy that space beside you, inside you."

"I'm tired. I'm tired of trying. I'm tired of fighting. I'm tired of getting nowhere." Emily could not hold her tears in and she sobbed into Anika's shoulder, tightening her hold around Anika's waist.

"Things may not seem to change with Conrad, but I know you are. Look at all you've accomplished. You've built a name for yourself in the editing industry. You have the chance at an amazing job, you have two well-adjusted daughters. You've found you. You know what you need to be you happy. If that means it isn't Conrad, then so be it. It probably isn't with me either. I know that. I'm just happy to be along for the ride."

"Anika," Emily started through her sobs. Sniffling she leaned back to look at Anika. "Why do you say that? That you can't make me happy?"

"I'm not what you need. You'll find someone who'll give you everything you deserve. I'm just thankful to be a part of your life. Whatever part I get to play."

"Anika..." Emily's words would not come. Instead she pressed into Anika, trying to commit to memory how their bodies felt together. Emily felt her arms tighten around her and she relaxed. Sitting up and wiping her tears on her sleeve, she lifted her head from Anika's shoulder and reached for her hand. Slowly, carefully Emily kissed the back of Anika's hand, the skin felt soft and smooth on her lips.

CHAPTER 15

Able to read Anika so well, knowing her better than Anika knew herself, Emily had an advantage. It was a talent that Anika both loved and hated about Emily. Emily could sense what Anika was feeling before Anika did. Anika was not a talker, nor did she usually confide in people. She shared what she needed to with her husband and mother, and bottled everything else up. Beyond those basic relationships, no one really knew much about the true Anika. She had chosen to let Emily in bit by bit as Emily pried her heart open.

"Are you okay?" Emily reached for Anika's hand, looking her in the eye. Calming herself and patiently waiting to see Anika's response to their physical touch, the kids came bounding into the kitchen.

"What do you need, Kari?" Anika yanked her hand away and turned to her daughter. Emily folded her hands in her lap and looked down at them in quiet contemplation.

"Can you help me get the Barbie castle down, please?" she asked in her singsong seven-year-old voice.

"Of course! Let's go!" Anika replied, jumping up from the couch, throwing Emily a look of apology. Emily shrugged her shoulders and smiled, looking down at her now entwined fingers in her lap. She shook her head, thinking that their relationship was becoming harder and harder to keep secret.

"Sorry, Emily. We need to be more careful. Karianna has been mentioning things to Matisse," Anika explained as she came back to the couch. Seeing Emily's crestfallen face, she added quickly, "She doesn't mean anything by it; she's just telling Matisse about her day."

"I will be more careful when the kids are around."

"It's not just you. I have to watch myself too. It comes far too naturally to me to be affectionate towards you. To kiss you." Dropping her eyes to their entwined fingers and her voice to a whisper, she added, "More than anything, that's all I want to do."

"I feel the same. Being with you feels like it should. It comes naturally, easily. Holding your hand is an automatic reaction for me. I have to think to not do it." Emily's eyes were sad as she met Anika's. The thought that their relationship was becoming even more complicated was daunting. They'd had more freedom with their actions with the kids around because they were so young, but now that they were more aware, and more vocal, the women would have to rein in some of their physical closeness.

"I miss you," Anika admitted. Emily, who openly talked about her feelings, had to understand the learning curve Anika struggled with when it came to expressing her feelings.

"I miss you, too," Emily replied, her throat tightening. Continuing to hold each other's hands, the kids played nicely upstairs. Emily tucked her legs under her, pulling Anika close, Anika spread her hands over Emily's thighs. Both women calming at each other's touch.

Sometimes I'm not sure that you love me, miss me the same as I do you, Emily thought to herself, swallowing the fear and uncertainty. She ran her hand over the back of Anika's and up her arm.

"I don't want to monitor how we are together, but we don't really have a choice if we want to keep what we have."

"I know. I understand." Emily met Anika's eyes through long, wet lashes. She resisted the urge to pull her hand away from Anika's; she suddenly wanted physical distance. She felt herself wanting to hide herself, but there was something in Anika's eyes that stopped her.

"Please don't pull away from me, Emily. I can see you doing that now. I can feel it. I love you. I have to be careful. We have to be careful."

"I know, Anika. Sometimes, though, when we talk like this, I can't help but remember when you said you could live like this forever. Me and you; you and your husband." Emily drew in a heavy breath, unsure if she should ask what was on her mind. Whether she even wanted the answer. *I miss what we could have been.*

"Emily, please don't think my feelings for you have changed. I still want you. I still want us." Anika kissed Emily's lips, gently, slowly. Staying cheek to cheek when the kiss ended.

"We have to do what's best for the kids. In all of this, our actions have to be done out of love, including the love for our children, and keeping what we have drama-free for them." Emily pulled away and smiled, doing her best to make the smile reach her eyes. Anika always said it was Emily's eyes that gave her away when she was unhappy. "Anika, would you be okay with physical displays of affection if we were... out. If we were a couple? Kissing? Hand holding?"

"Emily..." Anika sat back, positioning her body away from Emily's. "I don't know. Would you?"

"Yes. I very much would be okay with all displays of affection. I am a very physical person." Emily brought Anika's hand with both of hers to her chest to denote how deep her love ran.

"Yeah, you are," Anika pointedly raised her other hand toward Emily, then lowered it back onto Emily's knee. "I would be okay with it at home, but I don't even do that with my husband now."

"You wouldn't kiss me in public?"

"Probably not," Anika replied. Emily could not hide the pain that came at hearing Anika's admission. "That hurts you. I'm sorry."

"It's fine." Emily waved away the words still hanging in the air. "I just don't understand. What's the difference between at home or out in public?"

"People judge. I don't like labels. I know a lot of people in this town. They know who I am."

"Anika, what everyone says is no one else's business. People are going to talk anyways. Why not be focused on our happiness, instead of worrying about them?" Emily threw her hands up exasperated. *Why am I torturing myself by even asking these questions? We're never going to be 'out' together.* Quietly, meekly, Emily asked, "What label are you afraid you'll be given?"

"There are lots of labels people put on women like us. Dykes, butches, the list goes on."

"Does the label lesbian bother you?"

"I don't think that's what I am. I've said before that I think you're a one-off for me. Just like my husband. If I don't end up with you, or him, I'll end up alone. Staying alone."

Anika's dark eyes spoke to Emily's. There was a determination, a knowing behind the certainty there. Anika probably would never love another. Emily brought her lips to Anika's once again; trying to kiss away her fears.

* * * *

The kids played happily as Anika and Emily cleaned up from dinner and got them ready for bed. It was a school night, so Emily helped Anika out to her truck with her three tired children.

"Good night, beautiful." Anika embraced Emily

tightly, kissing her on her cheek as they released each other.

"Good night, sweetie." Returning to the house, Emily closed and locked the door behind her. After her girls were settled for the night, Emily poured herself a glass of wine and relaxed into the couch where she and Anika had shared their love. She had a lot to contemplate. Her relationship with Anika was becoming more difficult to maintain and, once again, Emily felt as though she was always the one trying to appease her partner. All she wanted was to have her feelings acknowledged and understood. All she wanted was to be acknowledged and understood. She was always looking after everyone else, and had no one to look after her. Emily felt defeated and alone.

Whenever Anika wanted a change in her life, Emily would make the necessary adjustments. When Anika needed space or when she needed Emily, Emily would comply, often calling and texting to reassure Anika. Most of the time Emily did this without Anika even having to ask. Emily was attuned to Anika's moods. She knew Anika inside out and did all she could to make her happy, sometimes to her own detriment.

Emily wanted just one person in her life to do the same for her. She wanted to feel that unconditional love. She wanted someone to know her inside out and know when she was lonely without having to say it. She wanted someone to tell her to do what she needed to do to be happy, with no strings attached; no worry that she might turn around and discover the ones she loved would be gone. *I suppose this is my failing. I choose to give that part of me to people. I choose to give too much of myself to others. She needs me, she has an empty place I fill. But I need her, too.*

Emily took a long swallow of her wine, playing with the charging cord attached to her laptop. She had emails and work business she needed to take care of, but her mind just was not into it tonight. Her thoughts kept returning to Anika. How soft her skin was under Emily's fingers; how her hair felt on Emily's chest when they lay in the afterglow of their releases; how her lips tasted as they brushed her own in secret on the way out the door.

Opening a new Word document, Emily began to type. Her words flowed endlessly as the tears streamed from her eyes and fell to her chest. Uninterrupted, her fingers spoke; silent tracks stained her cheeks and soaked her purple night gown:

Everyday I let my love speak silently,
The ordinary duties,
Your favourite meal, coffee hot,
A brush of your arm to let you know I'm here.
Yet to you,
We're still black and white.
You still find yourself in dark or light,
The dawn and dusk can't exist for you.
Protecting, saving, preserving,
You fight for what you need.
While I fight for the same,
For you.

CHAPTER 16

Emily was not used to not having anyone to share the big events in her life. She had always had a close friend to confide in. She was feeling lost in this situation with Anika and Matisse. Not only was it difficult to understand Matisse and Anika's marital issues, but, Emily was now questioning who she was and the direction her life was taking: a path she thought she had planned out, until recently.

She had always been open-minded. Someone with the label of gay or lesbian or any other word of choice had never bothered her. She believed that you could not choose who you loved.

Before now, she had not realized how good respect tasted. She had never experienced love with anyone that held a true element of respect. It was not just the way Emily felt about Anika or how Anika treated her. Emily's body had never reacted to a man the way her body reacted to Anika's touch.

"Anika," Emily began one evening as they settled down into each other on Emily's couch to watch some TV after a long day with the kids. Emily ran her free hand over their entwined fingers. "I feel like we're at a crossroads."

"What do you mean?" Anika asked, turning the volume down on the TV and shifting her body so she could look at Emily directly.

"I know you're unhappy with Matisse and how he's been since we've been together. I know you're torn over whether or not we should still be in this relationship; if you want to pursue it or the one with Matisse or if you have enough energy to do both. I know you feel you're being unfaithful to Matisse and that weighs on your conscious."

"Emily..."

"Anika, you don't like to do a lot of talking. You're okay with internalizing and figuring it out on your terms and in your timeframe. I tend to talk. I need to talk. It's the way that I get what is in my head, out."

"Emily, we agreed that for our well-being, for the well-being of our children, we wouldn't, couldn't, tell anyone about us." Anika became rigid. Her tensed jaw was noticeable even in the dim light from the TV.

"I know. And I would never jeopardize the lives we have both built or the well-being of our children, but I can't just sit here and keep it all inside." Emily did not know if her desire for Anika was a one-off affair or if it indicated her true sexual preference. Her entire world was changing. She was tired of being treated with disrespect and disinterest by her husband. She refused to stay in that relationship, though she did not believe she could leave until she was able provide for her children. But she was also being faced with a challenge to her sexuality and how she had identified herself her entire life. Men seemed, in Emily's experience, to all be the same. Some were different variations of selfish or unable to understand her but no matter the man, there always seemed to be a distance she just could not seem to cross. Women at least understood her needs. She could be close to a woman without feeling challenged or unimportant or insecure. She could not put her finger on the reason, but intimacy with a woman felt comfortable.

"I'm questioning more than just my marriage. I'm questioning everything. Since we've been together, I've become more aware of how I view others. I don't look at men the same way I once did. I realize the way I've always noticed women. I'd always been embarrassed by it, trying to hide my attraction. I realize I've pushed them aside. I don't know if it's just my curiosity, or if it is something more. Maybe it's just the excitement that being with you gives me. I don't know."

"Emily. I know I've been distant and agitated and emotional lately. You're right. I'm questioning my marriage and our relationship and my perspective. For me, though, I think you're a one-off. If we aren't together and if Matisse and I break up, I don't think I will end up with anyone else. For me it has nothing to do with being attracted to men or women, it has to do with the person and for me it is you."

"It was Matisse for you at one point, wasn't it? There haven't really been any other men, have there?"

"No, there hasn't. I take what we're doing very seriously. These aren't light decisions for me," Anika answered Emily, an edge to her voice.

"Nor are they for me." Emily let her hand go limp, tensing her arm away from Anika. Emily was offended by the implication that she took the decision whether or not to stay in her marriage or question her sexuality, any less seriously than Anika.

"I know they're not light for you. But, you will find someone else one day."

"Anika..." Emily turned, uncrossing her legs on the couch, shifting her body so it was open and softened toward Anika. Fingers still entwined, Emily ran her other hand up her lover's arm to caress her cheek. Anika kissed the back of Emily's fingers and brought her hand to her chest.

"Who were you thinking of telling about us?"

"I have a cousin who lives in Montreal. She is part of the polyamorous community out there."

"Oh?" Anika raised one eyebrow, showing genuine curiosity.

"I thought that she may have some insight on how to better balance our relationship with our marriages."

"Is she..."

"She swings both ways, if that's what you're asking. I've chatted with her a little on Facebook lately and she seems to be enjoying her life enormously. She is able to openly celebrate her sexuality, be creative and express herself without the fear of judgement."

"Something we're certainly lacking living around here, I agree. Call her. Talk to her. Do what you need to do to find yourself, Emily."

"Anika. I'm not going anywhere. That's not what I'm trying to do," Emily reassured Anika.

"I don't want to hold you back. If you have the opportunity to be with someone else, if you find I'm not who you need or want, then do what you must to find your happiness. I'm just glad to have been a part of your life."

"Please stop talking like that. If there ever comes a time when I need to change, then we will cross that bridge when we get there. For now, just accept that I love you, and let that be enough."

"I love you too, Emily. I love you more than I should." Their lips met, sending warmth through Emily's body. Emily stroked Anika's neck then entangled her fingers in her hair. Emily concentrated on the sensation of their bodies sinking into one another. Their sexual intensity was unbearable at times; almost combustible.

CHAPTER 17

"I..." Matisse looked away and his voice trailed off as he nervously played with the brown napkin under his coffee cup. "We need to talk. I feel like I need to explain myself." The desperation in his voice reached his eyes and tugged at Emily's heart.

"Does Anika know you're here? Have you told her what you want to say?" She tried to hide the annoyance and distress she was feeling, but she had never been good at hiding her emotions. The last thing Emily needed right now was to be having this conversation. She had been working on the last portion of her job proposal. Once it was submitted, she would know within the week if they would hire her. She was making one of the biggest transitions of her life. One that at least was a step towards no longer being dependent on Conrad. She had not figured out a way to tell Conrad about moving to the lower mainland, nor had she figured out if she could actually do it on her own, which would be her preference.

"I wanted to talk to you first. There are things I have to say. I need to explain my actions." An uncomfortable silence filled the space between them, despite the bustling café where they had met. "I'm sorry for the way I behaved. I know I've been controlling and my reasons for what I've done haven't been the most honorable. This situation has been a major blow to my ego." Matisse had taken pride in being able to pleasure Anika, something that he had not been able to do with Emily. When Emily declined the offer to be with the married couple again, Matisse took it personally.

"Why not include Anika in this conversation? We've gone over this before. The three of us could talk about it if you insist, but I thought I'd been pretty clear on where I stood." The door across the coffee shop opened and Emily shivered unconsciously, the cool winter air chilling her.

"Some of this I said before and I know you've… You've made a stand on where you want our relationship to go. There's more I want to say, more I want to explain. I don't necessarily want Anika to hear this quite yet. Sometimes she can be difficult. There are things about the time we were together I've kept to myself."

Emily exchanged the tattered, folded napkin she had nervously picked apart for the mug of chai tea she had ordered, but had not yet touched. She sipped her tea with her eyes closed. The warm, perfumed scent of her tea, mixed with the sweet smell of Matisse's cologne, caused Emily's body to betray her emotions. She breathed in, desperate for a way out of this conversation. She could feel his eyes on her.

"Matisse—" Emily started, finally opening her eyes with her cup still at her lips.

"Emily, I... Since the three of us... When I— we, were making love... I can't get you out of my head. You're there when I'm at work. You're there when I'm sleeping, in all of my dreams. You're there when Anika and I are together. You've stolen my sanity. I don't know how to move on."

"Matisse."

"I've never felt this way before. Not for anyone, not even Anika. It's never been like this. That's why I had the issues I did when we were all together. You can't tell me that you don't feel it too."

That's what Anika says. Emily closed her eyes once more and sucked in a deep breath. She thought about the intensity with which Anika proclaimed her feelings. Coming from Anika, it seemed more genuine than this almost public admission of Matisse's obsession for her. "Matisse. We were together once. I would hardly call it making love."

"I'm in love you with, Emily. I love Anika too, but it's not the same. She is the mother of my children. I've been with her for the last twenty years of our lives. I wanted to ask you to join our marriage a few months ago, but I didn't know how. I want more of a relationship between us. I want to try the three of us again. We work well together and complete what each of us lack." Matisse's voice broke slightly and he finally looked away from Emily, lifting his black coffee to his lips. Finishing it he placed the cup back on the table, but did not look up from it.

Emily's eyes searched Matisse's face, trying to read him. She felt angry at him for proclaiming his love for her without Anika's knowledge. This was most certainly a conversation for the three of them. At the very least, Anika and Matisse should have discussed it and decided on the course of action.

Matisse had no idea what Anika had given up or what her intentions were. Anika had initiated their relationship with the intention of enhancing her marriage. It just happened to blossom into a more passionate love affair between the two women than they'd anticipated, let alone what either woman had ever experienced. Not only was it a union of passion, but it also was one of respect and communication. The growth they experienced together brought them closer together. Situations which would have pulled other couples apart, forged a stronger bond. They worked hard at bridging the occasional communication gap. And since they were not allowed the luxury of unlimited time together, they made the most of the few moments that they did have alone.

Part of Emily felt anger, but part of her also felt pity and sadness for this broken, raw man in before her. Anika had expressed to Emily on several occasions that Matisse would be nothing without her. Matisse came from a long line of alcoholics and drug users; a line of defeated men and women who lacked motivation. Matisse would not attempt anything without her encouragement. Before he met her, he had nothing and was going nowhere. It was always Anika's concern that he would revert to that state if she left him.

There was no use in worrying what would become of Matisse if Anika ever left him, because that was not going to happen. As much as Anika wanted to be with Emily, she would never give up her marriage or the status she had: her privileged and predictable life. She would not risk losing her children. They, Anika and Matisse, were finally in a good place. Matisse's career was financially secure and they had worked long and hard to reopen their lines of communication. Anika naturally led Matisse, and Matisse fell into his natural response of accepting her guidance. Despite their differences, and even Matisse's sudden confession of love for Emily, they were destined to be together.

"Matisse, I'm sorry. Despite the passion we've shared, how high our emotions have been running, I just don't feel the same. I know what we've had has been intense. It's taken me by surprise as well, but it isn't going to last. You and Anika are happy. You have both worked hard to get to where you are and are meant to be together. I know that. You know that. Anika knows that. I'm sorry, but I just don't love you the way you need me to love you. I can't. Anika can."

"Emily, we can talk more about this. I'm not proposing anything crazy right now. I wanted you to know how I felt. We can work on it. We can involve Anika and figure it out. I think this is what is best for everyone. You and Anika get along so well and I'm not blind to the feelings you both still have for each other."

"Matisse," Emily began, allowing her anger to get the best of her. "You were an absolute prick to Anika when it was you having the issues that night. You don't trust Anika. You told her that we couldn't be together if you couldn't have me. How is that taking into consideration what is the best for the three of us? You are only thinking of yourself." Pushing her chair back and standing, Emily tried to compose herself. "You and Anika are destined to be together. I'm not part of that equation. Treat her with the respect she deserves, and neither of you will have to search for someone else ever again. She is not a hard woman to make happy. All she wants is respect and a sense of equality. When you're equal partners, your marriage will be more rewarding. Just work on your relationship, with her. She loves you and has given up, and struggled with more, than you will ever know, all for you; because of the love and respect she has for you. Without a doubt, you are all she wants. I also know that you love her."

With her purse in her hand, Emily weaved her way through the rows of chairs to the door of the crowded coffee shop, not giving Matisse a chance to reply. She pulled her sweater across her breasts, hugging it to her. She paused for a moment just before the door to let someone else enter. She felt a slow heaviness fall over her. She had half hoped that Matisse would come after her or ask her to reconsider.

Anika had, in essence, given up a life with Emily for Matisse. Anika was never going to leave Matisse. Matisse had no idea how close it had come to losing her and the kids. One of Anika's greatest fears, though, was that Matisse would take the kids from her. That aside, she had done some soul searching and made the decision, despite the issues she and Matisse had, to stay with him.

Anika had explained to Emily this did not mean that she loved her any less; it was just that she needed to make her marriage a priority. At times, Anika felt as though she was not being fair to Matisse, which would result in a temporary break from Emily.

The first several times this happened, Emily was devastated. It was hard to wrap one's head around the knowledge that someone could love and want to be with you so much one day and then be so riddled with guilt because of the relationship with her husband. Emily was finally able to make peace with these sudden mood swings. It was difficult, but also a great learning experience. She had to live in the moment with Anika, which meant making the most of the times she had Anika all to herself. What they shared, in their stolen moments together, would remain with both women until the day they died. They were a part of one another's soul. The relationship was one of discovery; not only of each other, but also of themselves and what they really wanted. Anika was able to find patience with Matisse and learn a better way to relate. Even Matisse learned that he needed to apologize for what he did and said.

I don't deserve to come in second, Emily thought to herself as the realization that she did not want to be with Anika part-time, finally sank in.

CHAPTER 18

"Dedrick! Enough of your ball-babying!" Anika yelled at the eldest of her twins as he scrunched up his three-year-old face, jumping up and down and whining because he could not find the toy car he wanted. "Go play already!"

Emily scowled and busied herself with the dishes. She tried to compose herself before Anika could see the displeasure on her face. As Emily turned around, their eyes met, and Anika threw her hands to the counter.

"What?!" she said, exasperated, raising her eyebrows in expectation. "He doesn't fucking listen to me until I get to that point. I always have to get angry with him."

"Okay." Emily shrugged her shoulders. At that moment, she noticed the muffins had to come out of the oven and she turned her back on Anika to take out the warm pans. In her frustration with Anika, she rolled her eyes. Anika caught Emily's eye roll, which just added to her frustration.

"Oh, okay, Conrad." The sarcasm dripped from her

words as she pushed the chair in loudly and started gathering the kids' drawings scattered on the table.

"Get out of my house!" Emily ordered. Hurt swelled in her voice. Her face reddened as she pointed to the door. She had reached her breaking point for the day, for the week, for the year!

"Wow!" was all Anika could mutter. Shaking her head, she stormed toward the back door, calling, "Dedrick! Dominic! Karianna! Time to go. Now!"

"But, mom—" Karianna started, confused and startled by the sudden change in plans.

"Now! We're going home."

Anika roughly herded all her children together. Picking Dedrick up, and towing Dominic in hand, not waiting for Karianna to put her jacket on, she pushed them out the door, slamming it as they left. Emily abruptly turned to the sink and started washing dishes.

"Mom, why did they have to go home?" Claire asked.

"Mommy and Anika were having a difference of opinion, so we're going to have some time apart." Emily tried to keep her tone light and even. She felt oddly calm, but could still feel the hurt and anger simmering inside. She was in disbelief that Anika could so deeply wound her with such simple words. That was the problem with knowing someone so well, you knew exactly what buttons to push; just how to hurt them in every perfect way.

* * * *

The day passed and neither woman had picked up the phone to call. Usually Emily could not stand the distance between her and Anika when they were fighting and would send a text or an email to try to end the disagreement. A piece of her missing when they parted on bad terms. Emily did not like having a rift between them, but this time she did not want to apologize first. She did not want to be the one to break the silence this time. Emily was tired of being walked on and called down. The phone interrupted Emily's thoughts. She picked up the handset and recognized Anika's number.

"Hello." Emily was trying to make excuses in her head, validating her reasons for kicking Anika out of her house. As the silence grew, so did her guilt for not dealing with the situation better.

"Hi." The silence was heavy between them. Seconds passed like long minutes.

"Emily…" Anika started, hesitantly. Emily remained silent, being stubborn for no other reason than for stubbornness' sake.

"Anika," Emily mimicked Anika. She wanted to stay angry but felt her resolve slipping. She did not really want to fight with Anika, she wanted it to be easy for once in her life. She was trying to make a point, but that was only causing more harm to their already damaged relationship.

"I'm sorry. It felt like you were turning your back on me. Mocking me when you rolled your eyes."

"I wasn't mocking you and I wasn't turning my back on you. I'm sorry I rolled my eyes. I was frustrated, but I was just trying to take the muffins out of the oven. I know the boys can be frustrating for you. I want to help you, and I try to make suggestions, but they aren't well received."

"I have to remind myself that what you say is coming from a place of good intention. I get frustrated, though. Sometimes your advice isn't what I want to hear or what I need to hear. It just doesn't work for me. With the twins. There are things about you that I don't like, but I accept you for who you are. I don't try to offer advice." Anika explained. Emily was silent, a mixture of contempt and offense doused in regret and pride.

"I'm not sure how I'm supposed to take that." Emily replied, pacing the kitchen.

"I'm not sure what you expect. You can't change me and you can't fix me. I am who I am," Anika replied quietly.

"I recognize you for who you are. I just was hoping to suggest some of the tools I've found useful. You don't have to get angry."

"I've always used anger to motivate me and to keep me from getting hurt. It works good for me, has for years. I have to get to that point with them. They just don't listen otherwise." Anika paused, then added, "I don't know if you think you can change me, but you can't."

"Anika. I never said I wanted to change you. You

keep going back to that. Like I said, I just want to help you. I know..." Emily finally allowed the tears she had been holding back to come. Her anger was gone, and only the yearning for her friend and lover remained. "I can see that you have issues you haven't dealt with. Maybe talking about some of it might help with the kids. It might make you less angry."

"I don't want to talk about it. Talking means remembering. The past is the past and that is where it can stay. I don't need you to try to fix me. I will work through my issues when the time is right and then I will put them away. I don't want to think about the negative. I want to be positive and think happy thoughts. It doesn't have anything to do with the kids." Anika's words trailed off and Emily could hear noise and scuffling in the back ground. Muffled voices and children's complaints met Emily's ears.

"Do you need to go?" Emily waited for Anika's response, listening to her raised voice in response to the twins' screams.

"Enough! I'm on the phone!"

"Do you need me to let you go?" Emily asked again, louder this time.

"Sorry. I'll call you back later."

"No worries," Emily reassured her, hanging up the phone.

CHAPTER 19

Emily was cleaning out her bedroom when she heard a knock at her front door. Glancing at the clock, always expecting the worst from late night visitors, she nervously found her way out of the piles of stacked books and clothing and down the stairs. Looking through the peep hole on the door, she saw Anika standing on her porch, holding a bottle of wine.

"Anika! What are you doing here?" Emily held the door open as Anika stepped in. They embraced one-handedly as Emily shut the door, Anika still holding the bottle of wine.

"I hated where we left off yesterday. I'm sorry about all of it."

"Anika..." Emily started, but Anika pulled Emily into her, pressing their lips together. Emily blindly reached for the light switch, plunging them into darkness, the only light coming from the hallway. Their kiss deepened, Anika pulled Emily's waist close and Emily found the back of Anika's neck, running her hands through her hair. The familiarity of their lips made both women stir with excitement.

"Anika," Emily breathed, barely a whisper. Foreheads together, both women closed their eyes, allowing their hearts to slow.

"I'm sorry I'm such a spaz. I'm sorry for not communicating better. I'm not used to caring what others think. I fucking hate that I care what you think sometimes."

"I'm sorry, Anika. I don't mean anything by it. I—"

"I know you don't. But sometimes your advice comes across as judgmental. Usually this wouldn't bother me, but then I find myself searching for your approval and, when I think you disagree with me, I get angry. I don't want you to think less of me. I don't want you to disapprove of me, or my actions. And I absolutely hate that. I shouldn't care what you or anyone else thinks. I never have before," Anika explained. "I needed to feel supported by you and I didn't."

"Anika, we can disagree and still love each other. You need to talk to me, tell me when you're upset instead of shutting down. I love you, sweetie. I only wanted to help. I will try to support you better." Their lips met again, slow and gentle this time.

"Thank you, Emily."

"Now how about that wine." Emily broke away, raising an eyebrow at Anika.

"Go get some glasses, sexy." Anika smacked Emily's ass as she walked away. Emily turned around sticking her tongue out teasingly as she entered the hallway, heading toward the kitchen. Anika followed, trying to smack Emily one more time. Both women giggled as Emily caught Anika's hand and placed in on her hip as they went into the kitchen. Going to her wine rack where the opener and glasses were stored, Emily removed two glasses, briefly inspecting them in the dim light; with children in the house, you never knew what their dirty fingers had smudged.

"How long can you stay?" Emily asked, hopeful. She knew Matisse was at home and she was curious as to how Anika had managed to slip out.

"I went to town to get some groceries and I told Matisse I would be a while. I have a couple of hours." The cork popped easily and Anika watched the wine fill the glass.

"Excellent," Emily said quietly, handing Anika her glass. Taking Anika's hand, Emily led her upstairs. The bed was neatly made despite the mess around it. "Sorry for the clutter. I was reorganizing."

"What clutter?" Anika playfully responded, settling herself on the bed and sending that smile that made Emily feel like a teenager again. Emily smiled back in response, taking a long sip of her wine, not breaking eye contact. She climbed on the bed next to Anika, their legs entwined. Between their husbands, work and family obligations, it had been too long since they had enjoyed a private moment together. Both women felt the warming effects of the wine, as well as the draw to each other. They needed physical contact. They needed each other. Both hated to admit the need they had for each other. It was not just a need, it was an innate desire.

Their lips met again. Emily gently bit Anika's lower lip and pulled away. Anika, eyes closed, moaned and gently sucked on her bottom lip as if savouring Emily's nibble.

Emily watched Anika's face as she opened her eyes and finished her glass of wine. *This is the woman I love,* she thought to herself, finishing her wine as well and reaching to place both glasses on the low dresser next to the bed.

Anika adjusted herself on the blue comforter, laying on her back and reaching her arms out to Emily. Emily climbed between Anika's open arms and legs, but before coming down on top of Anika, Emily removed her shirt to reveal she was not wearing a bra. In response, Anika sat up to allow Emily to remove her shirt. Lifting the hem over Anika's head, she threw the shirt to the floor and reached around, undoing her bra with one hand. Tossing that aside as well, Emily leaned forward, gently lowering herself onto Anika, Emily pressed her lips once again to Anika's.

Anika ran her fingers up and down Emily's bare back, giving Emily goose bumps. The feel of their bodies pressed together was comforting and arousing. Their mouths opened allowing their tongues to once again explore each other; something neither tired of doing.

Emily raised her body and traveled a path of kisses down Anika's neck, down her chest. Licking, gently kissing and finally bringing Anika's erect nipple to her mouth, she suckled it until Anika arched her back in pleasure. Anika quickly raised and suddenly Emily was below Anika, staring up into eyes that wanted to devour her.

"Take off your pants," Anika commanded

"You as well," Emily countered, reaching for the elastic on her own black yoga pants.

Anika stood beside the bed and started to removed her jeans. Emily removed her pants at the same time and leaned back on the bed. Emily's pants were easier to take off and as she watched Anika remove hers, Emily brought a hand to her clitoris. Anika gasped in appreciation and pleasure at the sight of Emily touching herself. Anika dropped both her pants and underwear in a pile beside the bed. Leaning over, Anika kissed Emily hard on the lips, leaving Emily breathless. Kissing down Emily's body, pausing to savor each tender place, Anika finally ended up where Emily's fingers had started. As Anika devoured Emily, both women succumbed to their desires that they had to put away far too often.

* * * *

Emily and Anika lay in each other's arms, basking in the glow of fresh release. Neither woman wanted the evening to end. They had enjoyed each other thoroughly and wished they could fall asleep together, waking up to the chaos of all five of their children. That was not how the night could go, though, as Anika had to be home soon.

"Do you have time to have a bath and finish the bottle of wine you brought?" Emily asked hopeful. Any time that they could squeeze out of the minutes they had together was precious.

"Yes," she replied groggily, snuggling closer on Emily's chest.

"I'll go start it." Emily kissed Anika's head and gently got up from the bed. "You grab the wine." Emily threw her robe to Anika as she left to start the bath. Turning around before leaving the room, Emily stopped in the door way and looked at Anika as she propped herself up on her elbow. Emily took in all of Anika's womanly curves, so different from her own. "You're beautiful, you know."

"You are by far the beautiful one, Emily. Not me."

"Anika…"

"Go get that bath started, would you?" Anika winked and jokingly tossed a pillow towards the door. Emily backed into the hallway smiling and padded to the bathroom, turning on the water in the soaker tub. Climbing in, she closed her eyes, waiting for Anika. It felt so natural to be with Anika. Everything seemed right when they were together.

"Hi," Anika interrupted, holding up the bottle of wine and their glasses.

"Hi," Emily returned, unable to contain the happiness she felt sharing these intimate acts with Anika. Sitting up, she made room for Anika in the tub. Climbing in, Anika sat facing Emily. They wrapped their arms around each other and pressed their foreheads together. They were a tangle of limbs in hot water.

"Hi to you too," Anika replied with a lopsided grin and kissed Emily's forehead.

"Thank you for coming over."

"Thank you for accepting me. For wanting me in your life."

"Anika! Of course, I want you in my life. You're not only an integral part of my life, but my kids' lives as well." They finished their bath and wine in silence. Both women taking in the sensations of the evening. The silence never had felt odd between them.

"I wish you didn't have to go," Emily spoke with emotion in her voice. Wrapping her arms around her robed body, she made an effort to hold her need inside, a futile effort.

"Me too. I…" Anika paused mid-sentence. "Do you hear that?"

"What's that?" Emily asked puzzled.

"I thought I heard a car door slam." Anika drew back from the window and pulled her sweater over her. Emily discreetly peeked out the blinds covering the window beside her door and saw tail lights parked on the road.

"Is that Matisse?"

"I don't know. It better not be. He's supposed to be home with the kids. They're sleeping," Anika fumed.

"I'm sorry. You should probably go."

"Text me later?"

"Always." Their lips brushing on the way out, Anika jogged down the steps to her vehicle. As she did, the car on the road spun their tires on the loose gravel left over from the winter in an attempt to leave quickly.

Emily's heart jumped into her throat. She was sure it had been Matisse parked on the road and it worried her. *How long had he been out there?* Emily thought as she contemplated what this might mean for little time they found to be together.

"Fuck," Emily muttered under her breath. She turned away from the door she had just locked and leaned against it. Breathing deeply, she went in search of her phone. She allowed five minutes to pass before texting Anika in search of an answer.

"Was it Matisse?"

Anika should know by now if it were Matisse. She hoped she would have a response sooner rather than later. Emily waited several minutes for a response before sending another text.

"Are you ok?"

Emily again waited for a reply. This time she did not have to wait long.

"It was Matisse. He wanted to know what I was doing at your house. I asked him what the hell he was doing leaving our children alone in the house. And said I was just stopping to drop off the phone charger I'd borrowed yesterday. I told him how angry I was about him leaving the kids. He's been very apologetic."

"OK."

"Are you ok?"

"I'm good. Just worried about you."

"I'm good. Thank you for tonight I will call you in the morning."

"Thank you for tonight. I can't wait to see you tomorrow."

Emily was lost in thought as she went to her bedroom and placed her phone on her dresser, plugging it in to charge it for the night. Sighing, she turned off the light and buried her face in her pillow. It still smelled of Anika. Emily closed her eyes, breathing in the scent of happiness and contentedness, wishing the scent was not just a scent, but a physical body next to her.

CHAPTER 20

"**Is now a good time to chat.**" Emily sent the online message with butterflies in her stomach.

"**Yep!**" Was the quick reply from Jessica, Emily's cousin in Montreal.

Emily picked up the phone, bracing herself. Propping her pillow up under her on the bed, she dialed her cousin's number. Jessica answered on the second ring.

"How are you?! It's great to hear from you!" Jessica answered, excitement in her voice.

"I'm doing great! Lots has happened in the last year! How are you? We haven't talked in forever."

"I know! I'm doing amazing! Things here have been a bit crazy, but it's all worked out."

"Good to hear!"

"Thanks! How are the girls?" Emily and Jessica were the same age, but Jessica had decided to pursue an education and a much different lifestyle in Montreal. She had never looked back. Although she loved children, she was not sure that being a mother was for her. Being an awesome, fun aunt, and making a difference in the lives of every child she spent time with, was where she wanted to concentrate her efforts.

"They're great! Growing way too fast, of course."

"They always do!"

"Yeah." Emily laughed at the thought of her girls and the energy they had. "If only I could bottle their energy!"

"Very true!" Jessica replied, then turned the conversation back to Emily's life. "So what's been happening with you? You seemed like you had something specific you wanted to talk about when you sent your message."

"Well, like I said, lots has happened in the last year."

"Right." Jessica's response was short but she interested and encouraging. Emily summoned her courage and dove in.

"Well, for starters, Conrad and I aren't doing well. He's not the person I thought he was when I married him and I'm at the end of my rope. I can't stay with him, I can't raise my kids with someone like him. But I don't have the means to support myself and the kids. I feel pretty stuck with him; in the situation. But that's not what I'm hoping to talk with you about. I met someone else." Unable to sit still, Emily went to her window and looked out at the rain falling over the empty field.

"Oh?"

"Well, it started out as one someone else, then two someones and is now back to one. I know that sounds confusing..." Emily toyed with the hem of the curtain, pulling off a stray thread.

"Actually, it sounds intriguing. Who is he?" Jessica teased.

"The someone is a she. Her name is Anika. She is amazing. She has done so much to awaken who I'd forgotten I was. Who I didn't even know I could be. It wasn't something either one of us expected. This is a first for each of us."

"First thing, two women together, or first thing, an extramarital affair?"

"Both, actually." Emily chuckled, finding the question, and the ease in which she answered, humorous.

"Okay... Go on." Jessica's voice held amusement.

"It has been quite the experience. I've never felt like this about anyone. She excites me in ways no one else has. Ever. She... This started out as fulfilling a fantasy for her and her husband. It wasn't decided when we were first together, but I got the impression that Anika intended us to be for Matisse. That didn't work out, so now we're having to pursue our relationship in secret."

"What happened with the husband?"

"He had some performance problems and didn't deal well with the ego blow that resulted. He wasn't very nice to Anika, and I decided that I didn't want to try again with them because of the way he treated her. I didn't think that trying again would benefit their marriage. I guess part of it was that I wasn't getting what I'd hoped out of the experience either."

"That's fair, but what is going on with you and Anika now? You say you've never felt this way about anyone before. What does that mean for you?"

"Matisse, Anika's husband, said that if he couldn't be a part of us then Anika wasn't allowed to be with me either. We've ignored his request to stop sleeping together. And, actually, it was more of a demand. We haven't stopped seeing each other, though. We can't. It's just too hard. We've learned to communicate in ways that neither of us knew was possible. The connection we feel between each other; it's not just sexual attraction. There is something else; something that has been missing in both of our lives for far too long. Not to mention, the closeness with each other's kids."

"Emily, this started out for both Anika and Matisse as an addition to their marriage, but continuing your relationship with Anika behind Matisse's back is problematic to their marriage. She IS hiding that from him."

"I know! I don't want her to have to hide from him, but his reason for us not being together doesn't have anything to do with us. It has to do with his bruised ego. If he was still invited, to be with us, this wouldn't be an issue. He wouldn't try to stop us if he was a regular or even an occasional partner. We're not pursuing this out of spite. We're building our relationship on the love we've found for each other, and to keep what we were both missing." Emily breathed deeply, laying back on the bed again. She tried to remove the desperation from her voice. She did not need to convince Jessica of their reasons to continue their liaison.

"That's fair, but you have to consider the consequences on their marriage, even on your marriage, should it become known. Carrying on more than one relationship requires the ability to balance and be intuitive to each partner's needs."

"That's what I mostly wanted to talk to you about. I know you're a part of the polyamory community where you live. I thought you might have insight into balancing more than one relationship. Communication, ways of dealing with the jealousy that can develop when we're feeling left out or alone. There is just so much that is new to me. New to Anika and me."

"I guess my advice would depend on what your intentions are with Anika, in your marriage and in your life. Do you plan to stay in your marriage? Does Anika? Are you questioning more than just what this means right now or are you considering the effects of this on the rest of your life?"

"I don't know. It's confusing, exciting, frustrating and exhilarating all at the same time. I won't stay in my marriage for much longer. Or rather, I will do my best to be in my marriage for the least amount of time possible. I've had enough and I'm taking steps to get out, to find a way to support myself and my girls. I can't leave until I can do that. I don't think Anika knows what she wants right now. She has made comments in the past indicating that she could live the rest of her life like this. She loves her husband still, but I fulfill a part of her that's never been satisfied. But I can't live like this. I can't live in secret. She has said, if I choose to pursue a relationship with someone else outside of my marriage, our romantic and sexual relationship will have to end. I'm a one-off for her, she says. I don't feel that way. The idea of more than one person being a part of my life just makes so much more sense than trying to expect one person to fulfill all of my needs. I fear losing her, at the same time. I don't know if I'm attracted to women now because of Anika, or if I always have been and have just suppressed it. I haven't had good luck with men in the past, but I still find myself attracted to them. Does that make me bisexual? Does it mean I'm confused? I don't know!" Emily sat up, exasperated. Nervously, anxiously she twisted the edge of the quilt, which had frayed and needed fixing. Running the fabric through her fingers over and over again, she stared at the blue pattern.

"Hmmm," Jessica responded thoughtfully. "Those are a lot of questions that don't really need answers right now. You might not have those answers for a long time. It sounds like you have a lot of personal reflection, a lot of soul searching, ahead to figure out who you were, who you are now, and who you are meant to be."

"I know," Emily quietly replied closing her eyes and sinking down onto her back. She let out a noisy, cleansing breath. "Right now, I want Anika. I think she is good for me in my life, not just as a friend. I think I'm good for her. I got a job and it looks like I may be moving. We won't have any choice but to abandon our physical relationship soon anyways."

"I think that you should continue your relationship with her. The way you speak about her, the way she makes you feel. Just trust your heart. She doesn't intend to leave her husband, she wants to enhance her life with the sexual and emotional experiences you're giving her. Those aren't acts of fear or jealousy. They're acts of self-awareness and self-discovery. If your relationship is going to have to come to an end soon anyways, why not enjoy the little bit of time you have left together. Just be prepared for what might happen if you are found out."

"I agree. Thank you."

"As for how to better deal with the feelings that come along with having, and pursuing, more than one relationship at a time, it's complicated. There isn't any one answer for it all for it all. Recognizing where the boundaries are, where you fit and where she fits, are good places to start. You have to remember, even though you may be done in your marriage, she isn't. That means you are both looking for something different in the relationship you have together. You are probably hoping she'll fill a much larger void than she wants you to fill. Take that into consideration when you find yourself feeling jealous. Jealousy comes when our inadequacies surface and make us doubt the person we thought we were. Be patient with each other. You are both new to this. It's a learning experience for both of you. As you said yourself, no one person can satisfy every desire.

Keep all your friendships. Other friendships than just Anika's. Balance is the key to making anything work."

"You've been amazing, Jessica!"

"I feel privileged you felt you could confide in me." Her smile could be heard through the phone. "If you ever have more questions about the polyamorous lifestyle, you're always welcome to come out here. I have lots of friends who would love to meet you and share their stories; their failures and successes."

"Thank you, Jessica. You've given me a lot to think about."

"There's information online as well. Either Google it or take a peek on my Facebook page; I have some links posted there."

"Great! Thanks. Take care!" Emily felt much more confident and secure in her decisions and intentions, though she had more questions about herself than ever before.

"You too! Good luck! And Emily…" Jessica started, hesitating for a moment.

"Yeah?"

"Don't overthink things. She's your first. She's been a first in many ways for you. You've been her first. Enjoy, relish, savor the time you have with her, but in the back of your mind, recognize this probably won't last forever."

"Thanks, Jessica." They hung up and Emily lay flat on her bed, the phone on her chest. She stared at the ceiling, allowing the stucco to blur.

CHAPTER 21

"Thanks for having us over," Emily said, embracing Anika tightly. Whispering in Anika's ear before they pulled away, "It's great to see you."

"You look beautiful," Anika whispered back, releasing Emily and stepping away. "I'm glad you guys could come!"

Emily followed Anika to the kitchen where she deposited in the fridge the wine and coolers she had brought. The kids had already run off to play. Conrad had headed out to the shop in search of Matisse, who was trying to get the lawn mower going. It was a task Anika typically would have done, but Matisse insisted on tackling it this afternoon. The women were taking advantage of a private moment together while their husbands were occupied, before starting on the margaritas. It seemed they never had much time together anymore.

"Can I help with anything?" Emily inquired, settling herself at the bar as Anika placed a glass of merlot in front of her.

"Nope. Just doing up some dishes. Everything else is ready to go. We'll turn the bar-b-que on when we're ready to eat." Emily placed her hand on Anika's bare arm.

"Sounds good. I missed you." Emily paused, Anika's eyes speaking to her, sensing that something was up. "How are you?"

"I'm okay."

"Anika. Something is off. Are we okay?"

"We're good. It's me and Matisse."

"What's up? What is going on with the two of you?"

"Well, things have changed with us. Between Matisse and me," Anika started, taking her hand from Emily's she ran her fingers through her hair, loose red locks falling across her shoulders. The long sip of her beer seemed to satisfy. Emily sat quietly, looking at Anika with encouragement. "It's gotten harder with him. He constantly questions where I'm going and what I'm doing. He says he hates it when I'm on my phone. I tell him it isn't with you, but I don't think he believes me."

"Anika—"

"He left our sleeping children at home by themselves to come look for me, Emily! He doesn't trust me. Doesn't trust us or our relationship." Anika's voice was filled with desperation.

"Where does that leave you then? Are you making a plan?"

"I don't know. I'm trying to figure out if it's worth it or not any more. The man I married, the man he was before we started this, isn't there now."

"I'm sorry. I should have thought the consequences through before I entered into this with you." Emily felt guilty for having come between them. She hated to see Anika suffering.

"I think some of this was coming anyways. He's always been controlling in some ways. Always needed to have the upper hand. He feels like he just doesn't have control right now. That's why he is grasping at what he can. He's trying to get back his sense of power." Anika took another long swallow. "Neither one of us could've seen this. That Matisse was going to get like this."

"Is there anything I can do to help?"

"No. But please, don't think I'm pulling away if I can't text you or talk with you as much."

"Okay." The hurt was evident in Emily's eyes. She looked down at her glass of wine, twisting the charm around the stem: a red glass heart.

"Emily, please. I want for us to be together. I can't have Matisse constantly on me and be able to be anything for you."

"I love you, Anika. Whatever you need, let me know. Just don't push me away. We need to stay connected, no matter what."

"Yes. I agree."

"It's too easy for you to push this aside. Push me

away. When it gets hard." Emily held Anika's eye, taking in the depths of the browns and how her freckles brought out the flecks of colour within the warm brown.

"I know. I'm sorry. I will do better."

Emily leaned in, embracing Anika. Anika returned the gesture then quickly brushed Emily off as Matisse and Conrad came back in the house noisily in search of soap and more beer. Anika turned away and busied herself inside the fridge, retrieving condiments for the burgers.

* * * *

I'm so tired of pretending, Emily mused, sitting on Anika's couch in silence, the heaviness of the alcohol in her head betraying her as she fingered the stem her almost empty margarita glass. *But I don't know how to tell her. How to explain the pain of pretending; feeling as if my love is not reciprocated.*

"God, I love you, Anika. I can't tell you, can't explain what you do to me. How you make me feel. I don't want the time I spend with you to end and yet the hours seem to melt away into puddles of seconds which evaporate with the sound of the ticking clock." Describing, putting words to her emotions, giving them to Anika, released the pent-up worries. Emily bit her lip. *Maybe the neediness, my desires, won't be so....*

"I've not felt this way, ever, Emily. You are my love; you are what I want. But I'm so afraid that you won't want me. That you will leave. Everyone else has." Anika's usually strong voice cracked now.

"I've felt like this for a while now, but I felt foolish and didn't want to say what I was thinking. I didn't want to be rejected. I didn't' want to be—"

"Exposed? Vulnerable?"

"Yes." Emily clutched Anika's hand tighter in hers and stifled a sob. Never had anyone expressed so clearly what Emily had felt for so long, as Anika just did. They were more than just kindred spirits.

"I feel the same. I was feeling that maybe you didn't have those feelings. That this was going to end. I worry every day that I'm going to get an email or a text from you saying that you don't want this to continue; that you can't be with me. That it just isn't worth it."

"I'm not going anywhere right now, Anika. I will always be here for you no matter where I am." Emily kissed Anika's soft lips with her own. Lingering on the taste of the lime, she whispered, "With all of me."

The whirlwind of their relationship often left both women feeling stripped of everything they previously held to be true. Anika felt especially bare, given that she could not seem to stay angry when Emily was with her. Anika had allowed anger to build an impenetrable wall around her as a means of protecting her self-worth, ravaged by years of abuse and neglect by her parents and others. Love had been almost non-existent in her life. Resorting to anger was the only way she could keep herself sane and out of danger. If she never let anyone get close, they could not hurt her. With Emily, it was as though she had no choice, her heart was dragged along for the ride.

Emily brought up Anika's deepest, darkest fears. Fears that she had been able to tuck away and ignore since puberty. Anika had never cried as much as she had since meeting Emily, and not always tears of sorrow. They were tears of joy and happiness, and some were of sadness; sadness for the loss of herself so long ago and sadness that they might not be together. Fear had often been a driving force behind her anger, but now, the fear she felt did not make her want to be angry, it made her want to try harder; it made her care what Emily thought and it made her want to try to be a better person.

"I know. Thank you, Emily. I thought that with all the drama surrounding Matisse and me, you might not want a part of this at all any more. I was afraid I'd lose you."

"It was strange for a while, after the three of us had been together. I think we're getting back to a better place, though. Does Matisse know we're still sleeping together?"

"No, thankfully. He stands firm that if he can't have some of you then I can't have you either." Anika screwed up her face with disgust as she spat the words.

"That's not exactly fair. Sounds to me like he has quite the bruised ego."

"I agree. But I can't risk losing my kids. He would take everything from me."

"I'm sorry."

"He brought up trying again. Actually, he brought up more than that. He asked me what I thought about us three being more than just an occasional thing. He wondered if us being more than just people who slept together, would make it work." Anika spoke with distaste. "We've only tried that once and I've told him that you are opposed to attempting it again. It's a difficult decision for me after the way he acted. And then he has the nerve to ask if we can all start a relationship!"

"Did he really ask that? After all that followed, his ultimatums about our relationship?" If Emily had not had a similar conversation with Matisse less than a month ago, she would have been shocked by his request. He had seemed adamant, just as both women were, that the three of them would not happen again, but obviously he'd had a change of mind.

"He did, yes." Anika's reply made Emily shake her head in disbelief. She played with her necklace, lost in thought. Both women sat in silence, their introspection interrupted by Matisse and Conrad returning from the liquor store. Anika quickly brushed her lips over Emily's one last time.

The jovial mood of the men followed them in as they set the second round of margarita ingredients down on the counter. Emily brushed her tears away and threw Anika an apologetic look before putting on her 100-watt smile and heading to the kitchen to refill her glass.

CHAPTER 22

"We were joking about it the other night," Anika said offhandedly as she sipped from her glass of wine. "We were fooling around on the couch and Matisse jokingly started talking about the three of us."

"Oh?" Emily replied, raising an eyebrow in question.

"I told him it was never going to happen again. I said it wasn't good for our marriage. It was intended to bring some spice to our eighteen years, to add something new to it." Anika paused and took a deep gulp of her wine. "He agreed."

Emily pondered this point, sipping her wine and feeling herself blush as the conversation brought pictures of naked bodies, warm and aroused, to her mind. Her thoughts wandered back to how the sexually charged evening had played out.

"It was meant for you; for your marriage." What else could Emily say? They were talking about the encounter as if it was not a big deal. Yet, Emily found herself thinking about it every day. Was she expected to forget all that had happened? Anika still did not know about the conversation between her and Matisse. She had not yet found an appropriate time to bring it up. She had intended to, but Anika and Matisse were finally starting to get back to a good place.

Emily was happy now, too, although her marriage had not improved. Conrad had almost completely detached himself from her and she was more than a little annoyed with his continuing lack of respect and inattention. It seemed that the more she ignored his behaviour and tried to take the high road, the more liberty he took with her time and patience.

"Things are finally changing for us," Anika confided. "Matisse is making an effort. Spending time with me and the kids. He's quit asking about us."

"I'm glad that things are looking up for you. I'm glad you have some hope for Matisse and your marriage. I know how important it is to you to make this work."

"It is important to me. But don't think that this makes you any less important." Anika leaned over and gave Emily a brush of a kiss on her lips. Emily was quiet, her eyes remained closed after the kiss. She was happy for Anika, but felt something else as well. She so desperately wanted to pour out her hopes and dreams, but wasn't certain how Anika would receive it.

I miss her more and more, Emily thought to herself, though she wondered if it were her own loneliness that made her long for Anika in the middle of the night, or Anika herself. But whatever it was that drew her to this woman who had helped her rediscover what it meant to love and be loved, it all hinged on the decisions of four people: Anika and Matisse, Emily and Conrad.

Emily had no intentions of staying with a man that refused to meet her needs, who challenged her faith and beliefs, who chose not to validate her. Conrad showed his disdain, his lack of respect and interest toward Emily daily. There had been no progress. He did what he was always going to do. Emily had to move on with her life.

Anika and Matisse were a different situation all together. They wanted to make their marriage better. Anika would have bad weeks; Matisse would have worse weeks and take it out on Anika, but no matter what, they continued to try to communicate in their own way. They strived to make what they had between them succeed.

"What's wrong, Emily?"

"Nothing, sweetie." Emily brushed the back of her hand over Anika's soft, freckled cheek. "What did you both talk about?"

"He brought up my going back to school, now that the twins will be going to kindergarten come September. He thought it was time I did something for me. We have a little money saved up."

"Oh! That is so exciting! What were you thinking of taking?"

"Culinary arts. It's only a two-year program, with the second year being an apprenticeship, and an almost certain guarantee of employment afterwards."

"That's amazing, Anika! I'm excited for you! Are classes full-time?"

"Some of the courses I can take online at home and I'll only need to come in for the practical classes. It's a great program."

"I'm proud of you!" Emily kissed Anika deeply, both women still smiling. "It's time you did something for yourself."

"Thank you! I hope Matisse continues to be as supportive as he says he is going to be. I'm going to need the help."

"You will do well. You can accomplish anything you put your mind to." Emily reassured Anika squeezing her hand and smiling.

"Matisse says he wants me to spend more time at home with him. He wants to spend more time with the kids when he's home. More family time. He says he's been feeling disconnected from me since the three of us happened. In his words, it really 'screwed us up.'"

"I'm sorry, Anika. I wish it had turned out differently for you. I know it has been a long journey."

"It's not your fault. We all walked into it knowing what could happen. It just took a turn for the worse."

"I'm glad things are getting better. You deserve better. Don't take any crap from him. Tell him what you need."

"Don't you worry about that!" Anika stated valiantly, winking at Emily.

"It's difficult to ignore you when you're determined." Emily winked back and gave Anika's arm a squeeze.

"What's wrong?" Emily had grown serious and as usual, Anika had caught it.

"Nothing, sweetie. Just thinking about everything I have to do and how excited I am for you," Emily rambled, hoping to express her thoughts before her fears took control. "I didn't think you and I had made up our minds as to what was going to happen with us, with moving. Sorry to seem selfish right now. I want you to be happy. I want your marriage to work if that is what you want. I know how important it is to you, for your children."

"Emily…"

"Sorry. I just… Sometimes it's hard to accept that you aren't coming with me."

"Emily, we knew that now wasn't our time. There isn't any way to swing this. I can't support you and your kids and you don't have the means to support the seven of us either. I have an opportunity to go school and pursue something I love. You have the opportunity to do what you love as well."

"I know, Anika. I'm not asking you to give any of that up. I'm just coming to terms with our reality. What our future may look like." Tears started to well in Emily's eyes at the thought of not being with this woman. Emily allowed her tears to freely fall. Anika reached out to embrace her. Everything Emily had kept inside over the last months was released in her tears that she cried into Anika's shoulder. She was tired of being strong and holding it together. Anika was the one person she could trust. Stroking Emily's hair as she sobbed, Anika kissed her head and they sat in the silence of Emily's tears.

"Have you talked to Conrad about moving?" Anika asked gently as Emily sat up and reached for a tissue.

"No. I need to bring it up. I just haven't had a chance to talk with him yet. He's home from work next week."

"We'll spend time together before you move. I'll help you pack. My kids will drive you crazy. You'll appreciate the quiet when you finally leave on your grand adventure." Anika grinned.

"I love your kids as though they're my own. The quiet is deafening sometimes." Emily's smile was one of sadness. Memories of the five children playing together flooded her mind. The kids were more like siblings than friends.

"I know how you feel. When your kids leave, it is as though a part of me goes with them."

"Yeah." Emily sniffled again.

"I'm going to miss you."

"Anika... I can't express to you how much I'm going to miss you; miss your children. You're the family I've never had. You've shown me the best of what life has to offer, what love looks like."

"Emily, you have done the same." Music played in the back ground, soft lyrics of love and loss. The women leaned into each other, their bodies once again finding the perfect fit between arms and chests, legs and hips. Swaying to the beat of the music, they comforted each other in the best way they knew, through touch. They soothed their grief with their fingertips and gave life to broken parts with their lips.

Emily found the hem of Anika's shirt and ran her fingers along the top of her jeans, grazing Anika's skin. A low moan escaped her lips at the touch.

Will this need ever leave me, this intense desire? Emily thought to herself as she brought Anika's lips to hers once again. *God, it's killing me, yet I hope it never ends.*

CHAPTER 23

There were times when Emily did very well at pretending that her life was good. There were other nights when the loneliness crept up on her and left her feeling so empty that she could hear the echo of her own heart within her chest. She did not want to be alone; really, she was not made to be alone. Anika was the opposite; she needed her solitude. Emily was better at accepting the circumstances of her marriage before she had met Anika. Before Emily met Anika, before they found love, Emily did not know what was missing. She knew that there had to be a better way to express her desires, but could not have foreseen how her vague longings would be fulfilled. When Emily and Anika started their relationship, neither woman understood the complexity of what they had between them. There were days when Emily could see the positive of everything. There were other days, though, when Emily felt as though no one could hold her long enough or tight enough to make the hurt go away. And that's what it was, hurt from years of giving without receiving.

Emily reached for her phone to text Anika and stared at the familiar name in the contact list. With a sigh, Emily turned her phone off and put it down. *She doesn't need to hear from me right now,* Emily thought to herself, staring out the kitchen window at the snow, reflecting back on their conversation last night.

As often happened with the two women, when one felt a need, the other would meet it. Emily's phone rang with the sound of a text message.

"Can I call you?"

"Yes," Emily replied. A few moments later Emily answered, looking forward to hearing Anika's familiar voice.

"Hi."

"Hey. How are you?"

"I'm alright. How are you? How was your day with the kids?"

"The boys were as challenging as ever. I'm trying to patiently wait out this stage, but I can't say my patience is holding up very well."

"I'm sorry." Emily's responses were short, reflective of the strong emotions she was feeling prior to Anika's call.

"Are you okay?" Anika asked, after a few moments of silence passed between them. Usually Emily was the cheerful, bubbly one.

"Today's been tough, that's all. I'm missing you. I'm wanting more from you today. More with you. Some days are easier than others. You know what I mean."

"Yes." The silence allowed both women to remember, to feel. Emily's heart felt full and empty at the same time. "Anika, my job... You're not coming with me, are you?"

Both Emily and Anika had considered the possibility of Emily having to relocate and what that would mean for their relationship. At the beginning of their love affair, they had talked about what it would be like if they were to move in together; to live together; to raise their children together. Anika had said that if Emily was to leave Conrad, she would leave Matisse. Over the past couple of months, though, as the reality of their relationship, their marriages and their finances set in, it all seemed like the adolescent fantasies of early-stage lovers.

"Emily," Anika started, emotion crowding her voice. "It's not that I don't love you. It's not that I don't want to be with you. Please don't think that. I have to do what is best for my children. I love you and I love your children. Emily, I'm sorry."

"I want to be with you, but I understand your hesitation. I get that you want what is best for your kids. I knew that all along." Emily composed herself, leaving her tears to stream down her face, but calming her breath so she could talk.

"Emily, I've never loved anyone like I love you, but Matisse is trying. We have so much history there. It's important for my kids to be with their dad. Important for them to see us happy. This isn't easy for me. I'm in constant conflict. I want to be with you, but I want to be with my husband as well. You give me things that he can't."

"You give me more than anyone else has. I can't do this on my own, either. I can't financially fund this move myself. I hate to say it… I need Conrad."

"Oh, beautiful… You know, this, what we have, isn't normal, right?" Anika raised her voice without intention. Emily's face flushed as she dropped her eyes to the cup she cradled in her lap, thankful her tears were not visible on the other end of the line. "Look at the other people in our lives. No one communicates like we do. No one tries to make things work like we do. You make me want to succeed. Matisse just makes me want to throw up my hands."

"Conrad makes me feel the same, but we can't base our opinions of all relationships on our marriages, especially mine, given the lack of progress. No relationship is perfect, but I'm sure there are others like us who make an effort."

"Matisse just shuts down. He says all I do is nag him and I never want to have sex with him."

"Sorry to be the bearer of bad news, but those are common marriage complaints. Men always want more sex and women are always nagging men to do more around the house. These battles have been waged since the beginning of time." Emily tried to make the amusement she felt apparent in her voice. There was never an issue between the women over wanting more, they could not get enough of each other.

Anika's frustration was evident in her voice. "He needs to back off. I don't want to be pestered every night to have sex. His mood is always dependent on sex. For once I don't want it to be about that." Anika had high standards and if Matisse did not meet her expectations, there was hell to pay. Emily wanted to feel jealous, but the reality was, despite the conversation turning into one about Anika's gripes, it showed that she cared enough about him still to want to change their dynamic for the better. Emily was happy that it was not over for Anika and Matisse, but saddened because it meant Emily could not have the open, supportive, intimate relationship she craved with Anika.

"We can't be the only ones to feel this way. We can't be the only ones to have found a love like this..." Emily's words trailed off, as she realized they'd always have to keep what they shared a secret.

"Of course we're not the only ones who love like this, Emily, but this, what we feel, how we feel, isn't normal. This desire is overwhelming. For me, this comes once in a lifetime. When you find someone else—"

"Ani—"

"When you find someone else, that will be it for me." Anika would not allow Emily to cut her off this time.

"Stop talking like that, for fuck sakes. I'm not going anywhere. I'm here, with you."

"Right now, yes. We're both with our husbands and our relationship is safe right now. But you say you won't be with your husband forever. For me, if you aren't with Conrad, then you and I can't be together. Plus, given that you're planning on moving, we won't ever even see each other. I don't want you to feel trapped by me, and I don't want to hold you back. You're a kind, beautiful, sexual person who deserves so much more than I can give you. Even if you were to stay here."

"Anika…" Emily began. "I haven't made any concrete plans. If Conrad decides to put his foot down and not move, I don't have much choice. He'd never let me take the girls and I won't leave them."

"You will go. I know you will. You must. This is your dream."

Emily thought back to how their arms felt around each other. She wanted to reach out to Anika, wanted to be there with her. The yearning for her was almost too great to bear. She sank down on her bed, pulling her knees up to her chest, trying to protect herself from the emptiness inside

"You will go. You need to," Anika repeated again, then added, "Conrad doesn't have the balls to say no."

"No, he doesn't."

"I'm sorry."

"Don't be. This isn't your doing. I never thought such a huge part of my life could be so bittersweet. I never thought a love this strong could..." Emily could not finish the sentence. The pause was long again, though, as always, they were never awkward. Emily's voice dropped to a whisper. "Kind of reminds me of us.

We are the bittersweet."

"Emily…" Emily could hear the emotion that Anika was trying to keep at bay, her attempt to be strong. Something Emily both admired and hated. Somehow it made this worse.

"We finally find each other. A relationship where we work together, communicate, co-parent and love each other the way we should: with respect and kindness and passion. And here we are, practically planning our goodbye."

"We aren't saying goodbye yet."

"No. We're not." Emily wiped a silent tear away from the phone before it dropped to her lap. A futile effort as her eyes seemed to have an endless supply these days. "Please don't pull away from me. I need you, more than ever."

"I will be here for you. Whatever you need. Just promise me you won't give up. Fight for this, your career. Your happiness. You deserve to do what you love. And it's the right choice for you and those girls. Even if Conrad has to go with you." There was little sense arguing with her. She was right, as much as Emily did not want to admit it.

Emily suddenly remembered her conversation with Jessica. This, her and Anika, was not going to last forever, but it was going leave a lasting impression on her heart. She needed to embrace it and take it for what it was. She needed to accept it as a lesson learned. All loves don't last a lifetime. It was an experience that had taught Emily a lot about herself and brought her to discover parts she had hidden away and ignored. Emily could not ignore those needs any longer.

I will make the most of the time I have with her, Emily decided. Out loud, she proclaimed to Anika, "I will take every moment I can have with you, until I can have no more."

"Me too. Now promise me you will fight for your girls and yourself."

"I promise." Emily felt more settled, more determined. Though her sadness darkened the light, it was still there, visible like the first star on a clear night.

CHAPTER 24

Rushing around, Emily was attempting to finish the laundry before her call with a new client. "Quit yelling at your sister! Use kind words, please!" she called down the stairs to her oldest daughter, tempering her voice to set an example, although as crazy as the girls had been today, all Emily wanted to do was yell. Control was not on the top of her to-do list right now.

Making it to the laundry closet from her bedroom on the top floor without stepping on any toys was an achievement. Turning the washer on and closing the lid, she could still hear the girls fighting. Hurrying down the stairs to see what the commotion was about, she came around the corner to see the cord of her phone pulled out of the wall.

"What are you doing!?" Emily grabbed Claire's arm and escorted her away from Julia and the wall where the cord dangled from the broken socket.

"I was trying to help Julia get her toy from behind the computer and I couldn't reach it. Sorry, mommy."

"You know better than to play around my computer! Both of you. I have a conference call in ten minutes and I don't have a phone now!" Emily threw up her hands and ran her fingers through her hair. Bending down to assess the damaged socket and wires, Emily felt tears start to sting her eyes. *Now is not the time to cry. Think...*

"Mommy, I love you." Claire leaned over and touched Emily's arm in an act of contrition.

"I love you, mommy." Julia chimed in, despite still keeping her distance.

"I love you both very much." Emily sighed sinking to the ground. "You have to do what you're told. You need to respect mommy's work."

"Okay, mommy," they both said together.

"Come here." Emily opened with her arms to bring both girls to her.

"Go play Lego or Barbies in your bedroom, okay? I have to figure out something for my call." Emily kissed both girls' cheeks and sent them trotting up the stairs happily, singing as they went.

The phone line was unfixable for the time being. It seemed the original socket had not been properly installed, resulting in the need for a new one.

What a time to figure this out! Emily sighed heavily again, still on the floor. Tracing the line back to her computer she saw that the computer wires were all still intact. She got up from the floor and placed herself at her desk. She did not have the client's phone number; they had arranged to contact Emily. That prevented Emily from using her cell instead. She opened her email and started to type out an apology with an alternate phone number for them to call. Emily cc'd her boss and hit send.

She adjusted her cell to full volume for both email notifications as well as phone calls and tried to busy herself with housework. Checking her phone nervously every few minutes, she found it difficult to stay on any one task. She wandered in and out of rooms, putting things away, but forgetting the reason she was there. Finally, the email notification on her phone beeped. Emily jumped at the sound and nearly dropped her phone in the sink of dishwater as she clumsily took it from her pocket. It was from her boss. He was asking her to call as soon as she could.

Emily took a deep breath and locked herself in her bedroom. Dreading what her boss was going to say, she could feel her heart pounding as she dialed the phone and listened to what seemed to be endless rings.

"I heard from your client this afternoon. You missed your call with them."

"I'm sorry. My kids were playing near my computer and phone line and ripped the line out of the wall. I didn't have the client's number to call back. I did send an email to inform them of the technical issue and to give them my cell number." Emily held her breath, anticipating the worst. Her feet fidgeted nervously with the comforter wrapped around her.

"I'm aware of all of this, Emily, but if you had been here, this wouldn't have happened. We allowed you to telecommute for the sake of your family, but it is interfering with the quality of your work."

"I know. I'm sorry. It won't happen again. I'm working on preventing this from occurring in the future."

"I'm sorry, Emily. If you're not willing to relocate, as we had originally discussed during the first interview, we will have no option but to let you go. We allowed you to stay where you are and gave you time to move because you were not only a good fit for the position, but the very best fit. I will give you one week to think about whether you can comply with the original agreement. If you decide to stay with us, you will have 15 days to wrap up any current projects, and then 30 days to relocate to the lower mainland. I certainly hope you are able to make this move. You're a valuable asset to this company."

"Thank you for being flexible. Am I able to send you an email within the week with my answer?"

"Yes, that will be fine."

"Thank you. Again, I'm sorry for the mix-up."

Emily hung up the phone and screamed into her pillow. Composing herself, she placed the phone on the charger and left in search of her girls. Life was too short to waste it on worry. The spring had been wet yet warm, and Emily needed some comic relief, a chance to remind herself of what was truly important.

"Come on girls!" Emily called, grabbing boots and raincoats from the closet as she herded them all to the back door. "Let's go play in the rain."

CHAPTER 25

"Thanks for picking those up, Anika." Emily's voice trailed behind her down the hall.

"Anytime." Anika wiped her nose on the back of her hand, walking heavily to the bedroom Emily's girls shared. Lifting the lid of the pink and purple toy bin with her elbow, Anika awkwardly dropped the armful of toys she was carrying into the container and shut the lid. As she stood there, arms folded across her chest and lost in thought, Emily came around the corner and bumped into her.

"Oops. Sorry. Are you okay?" Emily asked with concern. Reaching for Anika, embracing her, she could see Anika's earth brown eyes were threatening to spill over with tears. Anika was not always kind with herself and it worried Emily when she internalized her feelings. Emily wanted Anika to be kinder, gentler with herself; to see the woman Emily loved.

"I..." Anika started, opening her mouth. Shaking her head, she let her head rest on Emily's narrow shoulder, nestling in. "I'm going to miss you."

"Anika, I'm going to miss you too. Please talk to me. Something else is bothering you." Emily tried not to allow the desperation that she was feeling to enter her voice, but the sob that racked her body, and finished her sentence, gave her away.

"I'm okay. I… I don't want to do this now. Now's not the time." Tears welled once again in eyes filled with sadness.

"Anika. Please. Please don't shut me out. Make me guess what's troubling you."

"Emily. I..." Anika was someone who had never needed anything from anyone and made sure that extended to needing people as well. While pursuing her relationship with Emily, she'd had to admit to herself that she needed someone. This feeling of dependence was crushing and, though Emily was no stranger to this feeling, it was stronger for Anika. She could not handle not having Emily to herself any longer. She did not want to share her, even with Conrad. Now distance was going to be another factor in preventing their relationship from progressing.

Both women sobbed. Both knew what was not being said and it weighed heavily on their hearts. They feared what it would mean when Emily finished packing and left.

"I love you. I love all of you. I will always love you. Whatever you chose. Whatever you decide you need," Emily said through her tears. She thought she would have more time with Anika. More time to adjust to the thought of not having her. She wished that it did not pour every time it rained in her life.

"Emily, you have been my whole world. You know me better than anyone else. You're second to deciphering me only to my mother. I just..." She dropped her arms to her sides then wrapped them around Emily. Both women let their bodies relax into the embrace.

"You don't have to say it. I'm going to feel like pulling away. I want you to pull me back. Remind me, please. It's going to be hard, thousands of kilometers away from each other, but we'll try, and we'll succeed. We'll be okay." Emily held tightly to Anika's waist and cradled her head in her hand, gently stroking her cheek, wiping the tears that escaped her sad brown eyes.

"I don't want it to end either. I will pull you back," Anika promised and gently kissed Emily's cheek.

Emily already felt herself pulling away, wanting to protect herself from any more sorrow. But what choice did she have? Anika was the best friend that Emily had, she was a huge part of her world and there was no way around keeping her in her life. No matter where Emily ended up, Anika would be a part of her. She swallowed hard, holding tight to Anika, hoping some of the grief would melt away with the closeness they still had.

* * * *

Emily sat down heavily at her computer desk, cluttered with paperwork from bills to documents and requests from her job, all of which needed to be filed before she packed. The cursor, flashing where she wanted to start typing, blinked back at her. The warmth of her tea, minty and fruity, did not reach past her cold fingers and she shrugged her shawl closer on her shoulders. Tentatively and painstakingly, she placed her mug beside the keyboard, intending to type, when the phone rang.

"Hello?"

"Hi." The familiar voice made Emily's stomach turn with both happiness and anticipation.

"How are you? How was your evening?"

"It was good. Both girls went down easily. It's quiet tonight." She paused, hating the small talk, but seeing the value in it as well. "How was yours?"

"Oh, it was all right. Same as always. We read stories and Dedrick went to bed early for tormenting the dog and Dominic tried to wake him up when he fell asleep."

"I'm sorry."

"Same shit, different day."

"Anika…" Emily began. Feeling the pain of the words from just hours ago, or rather, the unsaid words. She felt as though Anika had left her, but in reality, that was the farthest from the truth. Anika was more involved with Emily than she had ever been with anyone. That was part of the problem; the reason why Anika needed to make some distance between them before it was the distance that broke them apart.

"I'm sorry, Emily. I didn't want to bring this up. I'm not an easy person to love. Please don't forget that we were friends first, okay?"

I'm not sure we were ever just friends, Emily thought, salty tears running into her mouth as she sucked in a sharp breath in an attempt to dispel the sobs welling inside of her.

"I will always be here for you. I will always be a part of your life, if you'll let me. Please don't take your children from me. I don't want to take mine from you either. They need you. I know you don't see it, but they do. They love you and your family. You're an integral part of our lives." Emily stood up from her computer desk, turning the lights off as she talked. Walking to the bathroom and leaving the lights off, she turned the faucet on hot to run water in the bath tub. The sound of the water followed her out of the bathroom.

"I love you mind, heart and soul. I don't deserve you, Emily." Anika tried to keep her decision to end it from her voice, but Emily heard it. Emily clutched her shawl closer around her body, trying to will away the physical pain she was feeling. Her heart ached, crushing her.

"I know why you're doing this. I get it. I—"

"I'm not in a position to leave here right now. Matisse is trying and even if he wasn't I don't want to lose my kids. And that's what it comes down to. He would fight me tooth and nail for them."

"He would fight you for all the wrong reasons. I know, sweetie. I know. Anika, I don't blame you for any of this. I love you. I want to be in your life. I will make this as easy as I can for you. I want you to be happy. I know I make you happy, but I know what you have with Matisse makes you happy as well."

"What about you, though? When do you get what you want?" Anika sounded angry, but Emily knew she was not angry at her, just at the situation. Both women had finally found someone that they could trust. Now their relationship, as well as the life each had built before meeting, was in jeopardy.

"This isn't about me right now. It's about your life. It's about making sure your children aren't taken from you and it's about strengthening your relationship with your husband so you can live happily together. It won't be perfect, but you still love him, despite the challenges. You wouldn't have so much guilt or be so torn if you didn't. Just tell me how I can help." Emily was desperate for some control over the situation. If she had a goal, a course of action to make this more bearable, she would not feel like running to her liquor cabinet and drinking until she collapsed.

"Let me be a part of this transition. This opportunity will define your career. It will allow you to make a life for yourself, and one day, a life without Conrad." Anika's reply caused Emily to break. She sank to the floor in the hallway and wept.

"I'm sorry."

"Please, don't ever doubt how deep my feelings run for you and your girls," Anika replied between sobs.

"Anika…" Part of Emily wanted to yell and scream

and tell her it was not fair. She knew that was not going to be helpful for either of them. Emily was glad to not be having this conversation with Anika face to face. Anika could easily read Emily's body language and that was not something Emily wanted right now. Emily played with the tissue in her hand, folding and unfolding it; creasing and un-creasing the soft, feathery material, flaking in her fingers. "Anika, there's something I didn't tell you this afternoon. I need to give them my confirmation by the end of the week. I'll be moving within the month."

Silence engulfed the line and both women sat contemplating the consequences of what Emily had just shared. The timing of Anika's needing to pull away perfectly matched Emily's commitment to her career.

"I don't want to stand in your way. I won't hold you back. You deserve so much more than I can give you. You deserve better."

"Anika." Emily's voice shook slightly at the feel of the name falling from her lips.

"Good night, beautiful."

"Good night." Emily hung up the phone and hung her head for a moment, silent tears wetting her robe. She stood up holding the phone, taking in the weight of it, or maybe it was the weight of the conversation which made her aware of the weight of the phone itself. She breathed in shakily, wiping the tears off her face.

Walking with a heavy heart to the bathroom, she turned off the water. Emily undressed, leaving her clothes in a heap on the floor. Climbing into the bath, she allowed herself to accept the finality of this heartache.

Try as she might, Emily just could not find it in herself to be upset with Anika. They'd had many great and meaningful moments together, and Emily knew how draining it had been on Anika to keep up her façade. Both women wanted to be together, but Anika still very much loved her husband and wanted to be with him. There were big changes coming in Emily's life; maybe along with the fear of losing her children, the fear of losing Emily had scared Anika. Emily sighed. Out of tears, she slid further into her bath, overcome by the thoughts she could not stop in her head.

CHAPTER 26

Emily had been avoiding Conrad, as much as she could while living with him. *I don't want him to come with me. I don't want him at all,* Emily mused as she absentmindedly swept the floor. Her girls were outside and their carefree giggles, as they played in the sprinkler, reached her ears. Despite her worry, she smiled at how innocent they were at this age; how little they knew of the struggles of life. How sweet it was to be a child.

Emily worried if she told Conrad she was leaving him, that she and the kids were moving to the lower-mainland for her work, he would try to take their children from her. He would not try to stop her from following her dreams, but he would threaten to keep the kids. If that happened, she could not leave them, which meant that she would have to give up her job. The one she worked so hard to earn; working in the evenings and in between caring for Claire and Julia. His selfishness would once again result in her sacrificing for the family they had both wanted. She had one other dilemma: she could neither financially afford the move nor fully support herself and the girls. Not initially, anyways.

Once again, Emily felt trapped.

"Daddy!" the girls chimed in excited tones as Conrad drove in the driveway. He was on day three of his seven home from work.

"Hi girls!" he responded going through the open gate, balancing the groceries he had in his arms. "Grab the door, Claire."

"Okay, daddy!" she responded in her little voice, excited to help.

"How was your day?" Conrad did not bother to kick his flip flops off at the entry, but shut the door with his elbow and walked through the house to the kitchen. Emily was still sweeping when he came in. He set his armful of groceries on the table.

"The girls have played outside most of the day so I've been able to get quite a bit of work done."

"I saw Matisse in town. He said we should all get together tomorrow for another bar-b-que." Conrad's response was not lost on Emily; once again, he had ignored her and her accomplishments.

"Sounds good," Emily responded curtly. "We need to talk about my job, Conrad."

"What about?" His back was to her as he unpacked the groceries.

"I need to give them an answer. They won't let me telecommute any longer. I need to go into the office and I can't be driving that distance. Both the girls are in school now so I won't have to worry about childcare if we move. They said they need an answer by Monday. They gave me an ultimatum."

"What do you want do?" he inquired. Conrad turned around and looked at Emily. She tried to seem as confident as she could, as she wanted to be.

"What do you mean, what do I want to do? This is the job I've worked for years to land. This is what I want to do. I have the opportunity I've talked about for two years and you ask me what I want to do?!" Emily had forgotten her resolve to remain calm. She had allowed her frustration to take over.

"Maybe you've changed your mind. Moving is a big change, a big risk. Is this what you really want?" Conrad's disapproval and annoyance were visible.

"For fuck sakes! Yes! This I what I want to do! I wouldn't have put so much work into securing this job and sacrificed so much if it wasn't what I wanted to do. Don't you see that?" Emily tossed her hands up then crossed her arms over her chest. She was trying to hold back her disappointment, her exasperation at his dismissal of this important achievement in her life.

"You don't need to get mad at me. I was just asking." Conrad shrugged his shoulders and returned to continue to putting away the groceries. Emily stood where she was watching him, arms still crossed on her chest, leaning against the counter. Biting her lip, she waited for a further response, for a vote of confidence, for his acknowledgement of the realization of her dreams. He continued in silence, apparently oblivious.

"Should we move? How do you feel about that?" she asked, uncrossing her arms and straightening, hoping a change in posture might make her seem more approachable, making it easier for Conrad to tell her what he wanted. He always left her guessing, though, left everything up to her. If he never made the decisions, then it could never be his fault if something did not work out.

"Whatever you want to do, Emily." He walked by Emily, taking pains not to touch her. Emily was left alone in the kitchen, feeling alone in the decision making once again. She had wanted him to be excited, to have a conversation about what changes would be inevitable with the move. *I wanted an actual conversation, not just an omission of responsibility.*

"I think we need to have a conversation about this. You can't just leave this all up to me!" Emily followed Conrad into the bedroom. "Do you even want to go?"

"No, Emily, I don't want to move." Conrad was annoyed with being followed. "But you seem to have it in your head that we're moving. Anything I say won't change your mind, so if this is what you want to do, then we'll do it."

"Don't you see how important this is to me?"

"It's not about you. Is it fair to the kids to rip them away from all they've ever known? Is it fair to expect me to find another job?"

"Conrad, it's not that black and white. The girls are young enough to adapt. We'll make new friends; they'll make new friends. And we will still come back to visit." Emily found herself pleading with this person, this man she had married, someone she did not even want to touch her, let alone move with her. She was pleading for support and acceptance. Conrad dropped his shirt beside the hamper and moved past Emily as she ran her hands through her hair. Following him back to the kitchen, she took a deep. *I can't cry now.*

"Sounds like you've already decided. Just let me know what we're doing. I have to give work notice." His back was to her as he poured the water into the coffeemaker and closed the lid, brewing his coffee.

Just one more thing I'll have to do alone. Emily glared at his back. Frustrated, annoyed and angry. This time, though, the anger did not feel debilitating, it felt liberating. She had followed her heart and found a love she'd never expected, and the career she had always imagined. This too, would make her strong.

"Great!" Emily changed her tone, standing straight, putting a smile on her face. Her icy blue eyes shone with confidence. "I'll go send the email now."

Conrad turned to her. Emily met his gaze with steely determination. She cocked her head to one side, arms crossed against her chest in defiance. Conrad broke the stare with a shrug of his shoulders and turned toward the sink. Emily went in search of her computer. She had found the piece of her she had been needing in that moment of truth. She was enough.

CHAPTER 27

Emily was in the middle of labeling a box of kitchen utensils when she heard the familiar ding of an incoming email on her phone. She put the cap back on the Sharpie. Stepping over the mess of packing paper on the floor, she reached out to grab her phone knocking over her glass of red wine. The dark liquid spread over the stack of boxes next to the cupboard and soaked the paper on the floor.

"Shit," she mumbled, turning around in search of the paper towels. Mopping up the mess with most of a roll of paper towels, she opened a new garbage bag and shoved in the dripping paper towels and packing paper.

Emily sat down in the middle of the kitchen with her legs crossed, her phone in hand. Turning her attention back to the email that had arrived, Emily opened the app. Two messages sat in her inbox, the most recent from the rental company sending her a copy of the lease she had signed for the apartment in the lower mainland. It would be a big transition for them to go from living in a house with a large yard and a view of the hills and countryside, to living in a crowded apartment complex. It would be an adjustment, but the freedom she would have far outweighed any potential discomfort.

Claire and Julia were looking forward to their new adventure and to setting up their new room. Emily had promised the girls that they could do some small potted vegetables next year on their balcony. She had researched their new neighbourhood and discovered a park and community garden just two blocks away. Plenty close for her and the girls to walk to daily if they wanted.

It had been difficult finding a place to rent within their budget. Because Conrad would not have a job when they first arrived, they would be making ends meet on her salary and his unemployment cheques, but those did not kick in for at least another four weeks, depending on how backed up they were. Their possession date on the rental was two days from now.

Emily was busy packing the last of their belongings. The moving truck would be dropped off tomorrow evening and then real progress could be made. Anika had been a huge help by keeping the girls at her house over the last couple of nights so Emily could give her attention to the final details.

Emily hastily read through the standard email outlining the rental agreement. The second email was from Conrad.

Emily raised an eyebrow at her phone as she saw the name. Her stomach lurched into her throat. They had not talked again about moving and Emily had continued along, following her dream.

Conrad never wrote emails. Ever.

Emily,

I know we haven't talked much about this move. You pretty much had your mind made up from the beginning. I've done a lot of thinking over the last two weeks and decided I can't go. I can't leave. I won't quit my job for you. You need to choose: me or your job.

Conrad

Emily stared at her phone in disbelief. She knew Conrad was hesitant to leave their home and his job, but she had thought he was on board with the plans. Two days before they were to leave, he decided to tell her he was not going.

How can he do this? Why now? Emily fumed. She resisted the urge to throw her phone at the wall and instead set it on the counter. With fists clenched, she screamed, a release of her frustration, her disappointment, all of her insecurities.

With calm deliberation, she picked up her phone and dialed Conrad.

"Hello," he answered on the second ring. He sounded composed, unemotional.

"What the fuck is going on?" Emily asked, jumping

right in, hoping to gain insight into Conrad's strategy. She began pacing the kitchen floor. She was angry and did not try to hide it.

"What do you mean?" Conrad asked, as if he had no idea why Emily was calling. Emily was enraged that he would play stupid.

"Your email," she stated, in a measured voice, trying to muster some semblance of calm, "Your fucking email."

"I never said I wanted to go. We never even had a real conversation about it," he continued, sounding rational while Emily was losing her cool.

"You told me to do what I needed to do. You gave me permission to take the job. I assumed that meant you were supportive!" Emily unscrewed the top on her bottle of wine and poured herself another glass. This time, after taking a long swallow, she put it out of the reach of her clumsy hands. There was silence on both ends of the line, no background noise reached her ears.

"I'm not leaving. I don't think it's fair of you to ask me," he stated mater-of-factly, detached.

"I'm not staying! I took this job and I am going to honor my commitment. I want this job! This is what I have wanted for years. I'm not giving it up for you. I'm not giving it up for anyone!"

"You're telling me your job is more important than I am? More important than our family?" Conrad was trying to manipulate her. Prey on her guilt for uprooting the girls, for pursuing her dreams.

"That's not what this is about. It's not about who or what is more important." Emily refused to fall victim to his games.

"That's exactly what you're making it about, by choosing your work over your family."

"You know what, Conrad? Fuck you! I'm going. The girls and I will be leaving in forty-eight hours. I don't want you to come with us. Your shit will be in the house. You can figure out how to pay the mortgage by yourself." Emily hung up the phone and screamed for the second time that afternoon. She stomped on the floor until her feet hurt, then ran up the stairs to their bedroom.

Most of the contents had already been packed, but she wasted no time opening the boxes and throwing everything that was Conrad's around the room. She made the decision that she would be taking the bed and dressers.

If he's going to be an asshole, he can be an asshole with no furniture. She grabbed a piece of paper and started a list of all the furniture she would be bringing with her and what she would be leaving for Conrad. She would have the kids, so the comforts of home would come with her.

After completing the list, she finished her wine in one long swallow as she reflected back on the phone call. She was embarrassed and disappointed that she had let Conrad get the best of her. But she had finally told him how she felt. She told him that he was no longer wanted in her life. She gave way to her emotions, the frustration she had been feeling for years. It was here, on the brink of destruction and madness, that she could start to heal.

Taking off her wedding rings, she twirled them in her fingers, rolling them over in her hands. Her friend's mother had once told her that if a relationship ever ended, you never gave back the jewelry because at least you got something of value out of the failed mess. Emily contemplated this advice, as she stared at the diamonds and gold. Leaving the bedroom and shutting off the light, Emily paused at the doorway to the bathroom. She stared at the rings that had held her unhappiness for so many years, then placed them on the edge of the sink.

EPILOGUE

Love. Our paths begin and end with love. Some relationships in our lives change and grow for the better; some become stagnant and bring us down to the brink of no return. All are meant to teach us. Whether we let the circumstances of our love define us is up to us. For Emily, love had always been bittersweet: passion paired with longing; desire paired with separation; patience with little reward. But, no matter the hardships, she had learned to care for herself. No process is perfect; it is the progress, when measured, that gives the true distance one has gained.

"Where there is love, there is life."

~Mahatma Gandhi

AUTHOR'S NOTE

We cannot always choose who it is that we love. Sometimes people and relationships come into our lives when we need them, but are not meant to stay in our lives forever. We are often accepting when this happens with friendships, explaining away our drifting apart. We hesitate to enter new stages romance and try to hold on to what once was. The truth is that many of us evolve from who we once were. In romantic relationships, that can mean we fall out of love with the one to whom we once joined our lives

I urge anyone reading this book to understand that you are not alone. Many women have entered a heterosexual relationship and started a family, only to find that they have changed over the years and desire a different kind of relationship and a different form of love. This does not mean you do not care for the person you have shared your life with over the years, it simply means that you have needs and desires other than what your current partner can offer.

Be patient with yourself. Be open with your partner,

if you can. But most of all, be true to yourself. Do not hide who you are because you are afraid of being judged or rejected. In the end, you deserve to be happy.

For more resources about this topic as well as information about me and my upcoming projects, please visit my website: www.vanessamthibeault.ca.

ACKNOWLEDGEMENTS

Thank you to the only person who recognized what was inside me as a child and showed it to me and made me believe it was ok; that I was ok. It may have taken me 19 years to find the confidence to act on what was inside, but you lit that spark for me: Thank you Kimberly Gillis Nashim. A big thank you to those who helped me through this process of writing and publishing my first book. I couldn't have done it without you: K.G., R.F. and S.G.. A special thank you to Transcendent Publishing for this opportunity and awarded publishing package!

ABOUT THE AUTHOR

Vanessa is a mother of two intelligent little girls who keep her on her toes daily. She is working towards her bachelor of arts degree through Thompson Rivers University with a major in English. She currently runs a daycare from her home as well as facilitates 0-6 programs in her community. Vanessa spends her days reading and gardening; making memories with her children. Vanessa spends many of her evenings with close friends enjoying good wine and conversation. She would like to travel and explore the world one day. She currently resides in Southern British Columbia where she enjoys warm summers and mild winters, where she can enjoy the outdoors. Vanessa also has a published piece in Transcendent Publishing's *The Peacemakers: Restoring Love in the World through Stories of Compassion and Wisdom* (2016).

CONNECT WITH VANESSA

Website:

www.vanessamthibeault.ca

Amazon Author Page:

https://www.amazon.com/Vanessa-Thibeault/e/B01MZILXQQ

Twitter:

@vanessamt2016

Facebook:
https://www.facebook.com/vanessamthibeault/

Find me at **www.goodreads.com:**

(Vanessa M. Thibeault)

Made in the USA
San Bernardino, CA
05 April 2017